D0661382

WE
HAVE
EVERYTHING
BEFORE
US

GIBSON HOUSE PRESS
Flossmoor, Illinois 60422
GibsonHousePress.com

© 2020 Esther Yin-ling Spodek
All rights reserved. Published 2020.

ISBNs: 978-1-948721-08-0 (paper); 978-1-948721-09-7 (ebook)

LCCN: 2019948033

Book and cover design by Karen Sheets de Gracia.
Text is set in the Corundum Book typeface.

Printed in the United States of America
24 23 22 21 20   1 2 3 4 5

♾ This paper meets the requirements of
ANSI/NISO Z39.48-1992 (Permanence of Paper)

WE HAVE EVERYTHING BEFORE US

ESTHER YIN-LING SPODEK

GIBSON
HOUSE
PRESS

CHICAGO

To Brian, Ben, and Daniel

"We had everything before us, we had nothing before us."

CHARLES DICKENS, *A TALE OF TWO CITIES*

AMIDST THE SUN and floral blooms of a Chicago suburb in May, Eleanor cringes at the bird sounds she has tried to eliminate from her life. From her balcony she sees the expanse of patchy grass and dirt trails her dog, Annie, has created. Across the alley in a neighbor's yard she sees the work of a real gardener, intricate arrangements of annuals and perennials, a gazebo at the center and, near their garage, a trellis with vines and tiny purple blooms.

Eleanor can hear the nesting house sparrows.

Once, pigeons occupied the eaves of Eleanor's house, and huge, stinking piles of their droppings had laid below. The uninvited pigeons cooed deep, low razors of sound before dawn, and flapped at the windows as if to stake out their territory. Eleanor would wake just as they began to vocalize.

They never woke Frank, her husband.

Eleanor couldn't understand the photographs of people in quaint European city settings tossing morsels of bread to attract these dirty, disease-carrying interlopers. She asked Frank to *do* something, explaining to him the problems of viruses and bacteria, worrying that little boys (especially her own little boys) would run through piles of pigeon shit then track it into the house. But Frank wasn't helpful. He said it would wash away with the rain. It didn't. Eleanor could smell the droppings from inside, through the screen door, a sharp ammonia.

Then an egg fell from one of the nests and left a partially formed pigeon chick. Eleanor donned surgical gloves, tied a bandana over her nose and mouth, picked up the dead bird with a newspaper bag and brought it out to the garbage bin in the alley. "Call an animal control service," she told Frank.

The man from the animal control service came to their house on a day that she and Frank were home and suggested a pigeon sharpshooter. "They always come back," he said of the pigeons. "They're homing birds. You have to kill them."

"You mean with a gun?" Eleanor said.

The man nodded.

Frank thought the man knew what he was talking about. The sharpshooter was booked for several weeks and he required a five-hundred-dollar deposit. Eleanor felt she was being taken for a ride and she could not hire a man with a rifle when she had forbidden her sons from playing with fake guns of any kind.

She told Frank to find someone else.

He hired a second animal control company, who placed traps on the roof and over the porch. As the temperature climbed to an unusual high, the sun warmed the roofing material and baked the squirrels caught in the traps, while nearby the gloating pigeons cooed happily in the eaves.

Finally, Eleanor called a roofer who suggested installing spikes to block the pigeons from nesting. "Same as under the train bridges," he told her. Spikes installed, they were finally rid of the fat, dirty birds.

Then the sparrows arrived. Eleanor could hear them even earlier than the pigeons. They were European imports, tiny bodied, possessing a puritan work ethic, and vigorously productive. They left tiny piles of sparrow excrement.

Now, as she stands on her balcony, Eleanor leans to her right and looks up at the strands of fiberglass and cellophane that dangle, woven between the steel needles of the spikes, the beginnings of yet another nest. Holding her broom, she climbs on a chair and smacks at the nesting material. Below in the yard, these crumbs float to the ground to join with the leaves and cigarette butts from next door's workmen, the puffs of dog undercoat extracted from the last brushing, and the sandwich wrappers, all prime European house sparrow building supplies.

Earlier in the spring, Eleanor had looked up to realize that the sparrows had built not only a nest over the back door, but that their sparrow community extended upward into the eave above the attic window. The colony now comprised sparrow mothers, fathers, aunts, uncles, maternal and paternal grandparents, cousins, second and third cousins, all not only flapping or sitting around, but dropping small threads of sparrow excrement, and an occasional egg (although not as traumatic as the pigeon fetus).

Eleanor called another animal control company.

Two burly men dressed in camouflage arrived carrying a tall, extendable ladder. They removed the nests and covered the eaves with wire mesh. But the sparrows returned through an opening and built once again. The two men came back and closed the opening but did not remove the nest. One lone sparrow returned, only to get stuck, impaling itself against the mesh as it tried to get back to the nest.

This morning the small body is still attached, wings splayed, tail at an unnatural right angle. It has yet to decompose, and its feathers flutter lightly. Eleanor leans the broom against the outer wall of the house. The last pieces of the new nest float down from the eave, but the dead bird remains, as if to remind her that the war is not over.

Downstairs the coffee pot is empty. Eleanor takes ground beans from the freezer and makes a new pot. She considers how Frank, who gets up first, never makes enough coffee for both of them, as if he doesn't think that anyone else drinks it. From the other end of the kitchen she hears a tight animal groan and the light tap of small toenails on the wood planks of the floor. She reaches down to touch the white spot on Annie's velvety black head, and Annie licks her on her knee in return. Annie always arrives when she smells coffee brewing, no matter who is making it.

Once there was no Annie and no boys, just Eleanor and Frank and a small apartment near the Northwestern campus. There were cheap dinners in the rooms of fellow grad students, intellectual and social camaraderie, and sparrows and pigeons could nest without fear of Eleanor strong-arming them.

At some later point, after her oldest son, Eugene, was born, intellectual camaraderie was displaced by more mundane concerns, raising babies, then raising toddlers, then pre-school carpools and PTA volunteer work. Then came long, empty school days filled with menial jobs; phone calls for the Democratic party, gardening at the ecology center, numerous fundraisers for worthy causes, until Eleanor could barely reconstruct the reasons why she had gone to graduate school in the first place.

It was not until Eugene was in middle school and was

reading an abridged version of *Robinson Crusoe* that Eleanor was able to put her earlier life to use, telling him that this was arguably the very first novel ever published.

Now Eleanor sits at the kitchen island of her remodeled one-hundred-year-old house, in one of the four chairs used for family meals. She doesn't always enjoy remembering the past before kids, but it pops into her head almost daily. She sets her coffee mug next to her laptop and watches Annie retreat to her crate, circle on the padding, and settle at the back.

Eleanor pushes aside the *New York Times* and browses Facebook for her upcoming thirtieth high school reunion. There are lots of people who look very different now, and others whose faces hold kernels of their youth and are much easier to identify. She finds Phil Anderson, who at forty-eight, in his matchbook-sized photograph at least, is much better looking than the other men. Spiked blonde hair frames a firm but moderately lined face. She is astonished at how good he looks. Thirty years ago, she'd shared a few classes with him, helped him with his homework, and watched as he dated prettier (though she is confident, not smarter) girls, and played on the football team. She had never been dateably pretty or socially outgoing.

But from a distance she had always admired Phil's looks and gregariousness. And now, well-educated and expensively styled, and at the very least an improvement over high school, Eleanor figures she might be worth noticing.

So, she shoots Phil a message. She wants to see if, like her, he has settled down with a family. She writes:

Are you the Phil Anderson from my trigonometry class? Where are you now and what are you up to? I am married and live in Evanston, a suburb north of Chicago, with my two teenage sons, husband, and border collie. Let me know how you are. —Eleanor

She rereads what she has written, to make sure it is simple and noncommittal, in case he turns out to be odd. Then she presses send. She feels some excitement, which is something she has not experienced in a long time.

2

PHIL ANDERSON HAD stood watching his wife, Linda, from the curtained wing near the entry to the sanctuary of her new church, while the minister preached to a stadium of congregants. Her look said the same to him as when she had reached orgasm, tight-eyed, flushed. It had been some time since he had seen her in possession of that look. In the front row of the church, right below the stage, Linda Anderson stood very close to a man not quite young enough to be her son. The young man and Phil's wife lifted their arms gently, fingers fluttering like long grass with the rest of the congregation, their faces rapt. In this postcoital expression, they both accepted Jesus Christ.

Now, Phil can't shake the image. It pops into his head as he begins his day.

Each morning in his basement he runs three miles on the treadmill, lifts weights on a machine that allows for rotations of exercise, and works up a soaking sweat for ninety minutes. He eats a high-protein, high-fiber breakfast prescribed by his nutritionist, bran cereal with fat-free milk, fresh fruit. Then he showers, shaves, and dresses carefully for work.

He thinks to himself that some might call this vanity, but his wife is leaving him presently. He will need to find someone new. He is forty-eight. He needs to overcome his age.

Phil's two daughters are both at school, one in college at Northwestern, and one still in high school. Linda has already left for work. Phoenix, a red-and-white border collie, jumps up to put her paws on his belly as he approaches the coffee maker. Simeon, the cat, is standing on one of the bar chairs at the kitchen island, his tail lifted, spraying the cushion. Simeon does this when Phil is around. Phil tries to grab the cushion but the cat is too fast. "Simeon!" Phil shouts. Phoenix barks twice, her ears raised and her tail out. The dog follows Phil to the washing machine in the hallway near the garage. I do not need this, Phil thinks.

In his Alfa Romeo, Phil reaches back and puts the top down. Phoenix settles, curled up in the passenger footwell. They exit the long driveway at the side of the house and turn on to the gravel road. Phil likes to check out what is happening in the neighbor's yards, and if anyone is outdoors. He makes a point of waving to prove that he is friendlier than his wife. The houses at this end of the subdivision are big, traditional, all similar, with carefully sculpted front and side yards. Phil had planted five weeping willows along the edge of his property and he likes to watch them sway in the light wind. He checks them each morning with a quick sideways glance, to reassure himself that outwardly his home portrays a sense of order.

Phil drives fast. Driving a racecar is the next best thing to sex, he once told a friend. He listens to the Rolling Stones on the radio, tapping the dashboard with his right hand as he drives along the river. He is conscious that he is tapping, forcing himself to get into the music. But he doesn't feel it inside.

There are things Phil thinks about while he is driving. First, there is Sarayu, the registered nurse he used to meet in secret. She would periodically travel through the area, hired by a health-care company, to maintain a certain standard of excellence in small rural hospitals. He had found her on the internet. She came to him once at his house, one night on a weekend when his wife and daughters were out of town at the grandparents'. She was long-legged and dark-skinned, and he liked the way she smelled, earthy and exotic (he had asked her to wear patchouli). He liked her movements, her thick, dark, straight hair. He met Sarayu mostly in hotels where they had sex. He wondered where she was now. He'd had to give her up when Linda had discovered the emails.

His office is quiet when he arrives. The phones are not ringing. The local economy is bad. Phil has time on his hands. People don't want to upgrade their copy machines or contract to have them serviced. Phil and Linda own the business where they both work. The only other employees are plain, over-weight women that Linda hired.

Phil sits at his computer in the storefront office, compos-ing new, lower bids for business. It is difficult to concentrate. Beyond the front window the sun is bouncing off car metal. Across the street the river looks cool and inviting.

When she came to his house, he and Sarayu had walked along the streets of his neighborhood in the dark. At the edge of the river, she had removed her dress and waded into the water. Her skin had looked pale in the thinly lit darkness as she floated on her back, her dark hair glistening with the min-imal moonlight against her head, her breasts floating above her body, evenly round and buoyant. She brought some of the pungent earthen smell of the river out of the water as she left it and kissed him, and tried to convince him to join her. He began to remove his shoes and socks, but better judgment took hold of him. They were still close to his neighborhood, and though it was very dark, he was afraid that a neighbor would see them. He was afraid he would lose the sense of exotic adventure.

Phil finds it easy to think about other women when his wife doesn't think about him. Even easier when the other women let you know how much they think about you. Sarayu was articulate in her emails, even poetic. She was younger, unmarried, and spent a lot of time on the road. She logged on to her computer every day. And she wrote to him. So, how could he not write back? And with summer almost here, and the possibility of her passing through town, how could he not think about her again? Would she pass through town? Would he run into her? Now that he was virtually free of his wife? He could go online and find her.

Phoenix noses Phil's hip through the side of his chair. She senses that the weather is good for going outside. Phil quickly gives in. "We are headed out for a walk," he tells Jan, the office manager. "You can reach me on my cell." Jan smiles and nods. Linda is out on service calls and Phil hopes that while he is out, his wife will check in and leave again and he won't have to see her.

Outside, Phoenix takes the Frisbee in her mouth. She looks up at Phil as they cross the street in front of his storefront to the park along the river. He throws the disc, underhand, toward the trees and the pathway, and she runs for it, diving into the grass to take it up in her mouth, running to bring it back. She props her torso up on her elbows in a low bow, and shakes the disc, then stops to look up at Phil. She noses him in the leg before dropping it at his feet. Her ears are pricked, her mouth is open, and she is panting eagerly. He throws it again in the same manner. He remembers tossing a Frisbee on the quadrangle in college, throwing it underhanded so that he looked like he knew what he was doing. Phoenix chases her disc again.

The day is pleasant and he is in short sleeves and can feel the sun on his pale forearms. He moves under the shade of a broad tree to protect his fair skin—his face, his white-haired arms. It is cooler under the tree. His brain continues to work through the issue of finding a new woman. As Phoenix again runs for the disc, he throws it back, but he hardly pays attention to what he is doing.

Later in the day, he drives home along the river with Phoenix in the passenger seat and the top down. It is a slower commute than usual because the spring and summer road repairs have begun in the last few days. He stops at the supermarket, closes the top to his convertible, and leaves Phoenix to protect the car with an open window. He picks up hamburger meat, lettuce, onions, tomatoes, and his favorite bottled beer, basic dinner supplies. Before unpacking them at home, he has opened his first beer. It isn't his usual drink, he prefers red wine, but he is thirsty. Phoenix sits next to where he is standing, her white paw poking his calf.

How can you spend years with someone and then decide—just like that—that it is over, that you must split your family and your belongings? He looks down at the dog. "How can you do that?" he says, without realizing he has spoken out loud.

He had met Linda at a fraternity party in college. She was a tall, virginal girl with long, dirty blonde hair parted in the middle so that it fell evenly over her face and shoulders when she bent down. Her skin was a pale yellow more than pink. She put up a protest when he first tried to touch her. So, he campaigned to get her into bed, and for a while it was all that he could think about.

After the birth of their first daughter, when he was in the marines and they were stationed in Southern California, he bought a large sailboat. As a family, they would put their daughter in a life jacket, slather her white Scandinavian skin with sunscreen, and set sail. Phil would guide the boat, and Linda would watch their child. This was when his wife was at her most beautiful. Not the night at the fraternity party, before he had realized what a challenge she would turn out to be. She had matured and the twenty-year-old baby fat had vanished from around her cheeks. She had colored her hair a truer blonde. Now she was an attractive woman, and they were an attractive couple. When he watched her touch the baby, putting sunscreen on her pink-white shoulders, dressing her in a sun hat and tiny pastel-pink sunglasses, this was when he was happiest.

Phil thought his wife spent too much time with the children when they were young, planning and doing activities with them, playing with them and disregarding his needs—not that he had many needs, or that the children were not important. Because he knew that they were, as he knew that they should be the focus of her life, and his.

When he was at home, she was focused on the children. When he was away on assignment in another country, well, he was far away. Then back again, then far away. When the children were young, they did not talk to him, but instead grabbed indiscriminately at his face with their tiny hands when he tried to hold them. They had smells that he didn't recognize. They were needy in ways he didn't understand.

He looks down at Phoenix, who is standing at his feet, still. "It's hard to have more than one needy person in a marriage," he tells the dog. And she lowers herself to a down position, ears pricked, head cocked, as though giving up, but still ready for a morsel of food to drop. When he begins to unpack the food, she flattens her ears against the sides of her head and rests her cheek on her outstretched paws. This is not the time he usually tosses food. "Even worse with two needy kids and one needy husband. It doesn't work. Maybe she didn't have it in her to pay attention to all of us."

He knows that Linda rarely even took care of herself back then. By the time their second daughter arrived, she could not be bothered to do her hair or put on nice clothes. He was away for months at a time, and perhaps she expected him to help with the children more when he came back, so that maybe then she could get her hair done or go shopping. But she never seemed to want him to help.

"Maybe Jesus will take care of her now," he says out loud, watching to see if Phoenix will move her ears at the word "Jesus." But she does not.

Jesus and the younger man, Phil thinks to himself.

Phil is not sure if Linda has slept with this guy. She doesn't really like sex—which doesn't make any sense to him—so the chances are they haven't slept together. Phil is a man who has never in his life had any difficulty turning the head of a woman, married or not. Now Linda has dropped him for this younger, doughy, plainly dressed and less attractive man who will pray with her. Phil bit his lower lip over the humiliation.

His daughter is not home yet. His wife is not home yet.

In the kitchen Phil forms patties out of the hamburger meat. He slices the tomatoes and onions and arranges them neatly on a plate and puts them into the refrigerator. He fills the sink with soapy water to soak the dishes, wipes the counter, and drinks his beer.

He opens up his laptop and goes to Facebook, where he discovers a message for him from an old high school friend. "Remember me?" Messages like this have been appearing regularly because his thirtieth high school reunion is happening over the summer. It isn't something he had been planning to attend, and many of the email messages he's received are from people he doesn't recognize. But this particular message is from a name he does vaguely remember, and the face, small as it is in the profile picture, is interesting, attractive even. She looks young for their age. He wonders if the picture is current, and what the rest of her looks like. He is intrigued but cannot form an image of her from when they were eighteen.

As though she is trying to catch him in an act of infidelity, Linda sends him a text. "At church with Albert," she says. So, she isn't prying to see if he is cheating. She is throwing her own infidelity in his face. Standing in the hallway near the front door, he looks into the mirror over the small table where he had put down his phone. He curls his lip. He has not realized, until now, what his face looks like when he feels such humiliation, and the reflection horrifies him. Why is she telling him that she is with *Albert*?

Phil is no longer preparing the family meal. Instead he cooks two of the hamburger patties in a frying pan on the stove. One of them he lays on a bun with onions, lettuce and tomatoes. The other he puts in a glass bowl and places on the floor for Phoenix, who is not used to such delicacies. Together the two of them eat in silence

Back at his computer, he rereads the message from the girl he used to know. "I'm married and live in Evanston."

He looks at Phoenix, who is at his feet as he types on his laptop, sitting at the kitchen island. After the luxurious meal, she has spread her body out on its side and is fast asleep. He begins to write and write. After forty-five minutes, he looks up to see that it is dark outside. He can only sense the hum of the air conditioner as it turns on and off, and the buzz of the refrigerator, sounds he once found comforting. He has excerpted part of his story, why he left the marines to live where he could raise his daughters, how he bought a business and now lives in a small town west of Chicago, about an hour and a half from where she lives. And then the hook, that he, too, has a border collie. Writing about himself is an exhausting effort.

After pressing send, he puts his beer bottle in the recycling bin, washes the dishes, and lies down on the couch to flip channels on the television. Within ten minutes he is asleep and dreaming. He is back on the football field in high school and the girl he has made contact with is sitting in the bleachers watching him. He remains on the couch all night. Later his wife and his younger daughter enter the house and take themselves to bed without waking him.

3

THE SOUND OF hammering has become unbearable for Kaye. She has finished her second Macallan's and is sucking on the scotch-coated ice cubes. Sitting on the back steps, playing with the ice in her mouth, she watches over the newly mowed lawn to the garage where her husband, Eric, and her seventeen-year-old daughter, Clara, are building a boat. Boatbuilding is something they do easily without her. Kaye grew up far from water, in landlocked East Central Illinois. She knows nothing about boats.

How many times have Eleanor and her other friends told her that teenagers fight the most with the parent of the same sex? Does this make the fuck-you-moms feel any better? Clara abandons her mother at every possible interaction, which Kaye feels is unwarranted. Frequently, Clara will run out to the garage, refusing to speak, or to help in the house. Kaye does not understand Clara. Clara's personality is one hundred and eighty degrees different from what Kaye's was at that age.

Clara has a busy and full life that Kaye envies. She has boyfriends. She loves junk food, pop music, and fashion. She starves herself to fit into tight jeans. She sings in the shower.

Kaye sips the melted ice from her highball glass. She watches as the empty tire swing that hangs from the cotton-wood tree sways with the wind. Once, Clara and her friends spent a lot of time on this swing. Now, they hide in Clara's room, or they leave the house and wander the neighborhood.

Clara goes to her father for advice. He is less questioning, less judgmental. And he laughs. Sometimes Kaye can hear his booming laugh from the garage across the back lawn. Clara can work alongside her dad without persecution, without questions about whom she is with and what she does in her spare time.

Eric had said, "Could you please stop doing that?" when Kaye reminded him of the exam Clara needed to study for, and her math homework, and the chores she was supposed to do.

And Kaye had said, "She needs to take care of herself and be responsible."

"And learning to work power tools isn't learning to take care of yourself?"

Kaye couldn't tell if he was being serious. "She has home-work."

"Which she can do later."

Kaye turned away. "I just want her to empty the fucking dishwasher and put her clothes away before she goes to have fun! Is that too much to ask?" But by this point, Eric had entered the garage, turned on the table saw, and was unable to hear his wife.

Kaye takes the last whisky-coated ice cube between her fingers and puts it in her mouth. The sweetness quickly fades.

Today, the temperature outside was warm, but now Kaye can feel the cool coming in from Lake Michigan, a mile-and-a-half away. Usually it floats in a traveling mist, the cold air mixing with the warm, which hovers near the street. As evening progresses and the light in the sky wanes, the garage windows begin to glow steadily and grey shadows move behind the frosted glass. Kaye thinks of the spiders and the mice that live in the corners and cracks of the garage floor. She involuntarily twitches as she moves through the double doors at the back of the house, into the family room. She pads quietly through the dark hallway into the kitchen.

There, she thinks about preparing dinner, though it's late. She remembers dating Eric in graduate school, then following him to Scotland, to a suburb of Edinburgh to meet his parents. She'd had more energy then. They had taken a standby flight to London, and then transferred to a high-speed train north for another five hours. It had been a dank summer. Her feet were always cold and it was always raining. Eric's parents set them up in his boyhood bedroom and they shared his single bed. Eric was an adventure. He was fast-talking, loud, and enthusiastic. Now he is bossy. Now he spends all of his spare time building a boat.

In the beginning, Eric had impressed her with his ability to absorb everything around him. At some point in their courtship he revealed his love of Viking culture. This in turn manifested in a liking for Scandinavian cuisine. Eric and Kaye and five more graduate students would work all night then pile into an old Honda Civic and drive to Andersonville, for Swedish pancakes and cinnamon rolls, crowding around a table at a place that offered large portions at a cheap price. At these times Eric made Kaye laugh so hard that she forgot her fatigue.

Now, years later, Eric keeps himself busy and separated

from his wife, a Scandinavian cooking class one summer, a kayak trip another summer. Kaye now experiences his gregariousness as overwhelming, where once she thought it a useful quality to balance out her own shyness. It was entertaining. Now she knows all of his jokes. In the garage with Clara, he can talk all he wants. Kaye doubts Clara listens. But, maybe she does.

Kaye draws a corkscrew from the utility drawer and takes an unopened bottle of white wine from the refrigerator. Thank God, she tells herself, for the small mercy of wine. She drinks a glass while chopping garlic, squeezing limes, and pouring olive oil into a large plastic container with the chicken breasts. Alcohol takes the bitterness from her life, helps her to speak out where once she was shy. She places the chicken container in the fridge and takes out a tomato and some lettuce to make a salad. Sometimes she feels she can perform these tasks in her sleep.

WHEN KAYE OPENS the garage door and asks her husband and daughter when they will be ready for dinner, they say they don't know. So, she closes the door and walks silently away. In the light of the patio, she cooks the chicken on the gas grill. She pours another glass of wine from the bottle she has brought outside.

The chicken and salad are good. Kaye knows she is a good cook. In the years of her marriage she has moved far beyond frying ground beef and adding canned soup and frozen vegetables. She sits on the couch in the family room with her dinner plate and her wine.

She wakes up at the hint of dawn, at least she thinks it's dawn. As she comes to, she realizes that it is her neighbor's backyard floodlights. Someone has covered her in an old quilt that had belonged to her grandmother. The quilt is soft from years of giving comfort. Kaye keeps it in the back of the coat closet and she doesn't remember how it came to cover her. Her mouth is dry, furry, and she tries to hack a cough to relieve it, unsuccessfully. Vaguely, she begins to put together the scenario of the night, the lights on in the garage, her late dinner alone, finishing the bottle of wine and falling asleep on the couch. In the kitchen she finds that her dishes have been cleaned and that the remains of the grilled chicken are in a container in the refrigerator. Had Eric and Clara eaten? She assumes so but she is too tired to check inside the container. Her head throbs and her legs are stiff as she climbs the stairs to the bedroom she shares with Eric. His body forms a mound under the comforter. She lies far away from him, on top of the blanket, in her clothes. She drifts back to sleep, not touching him. She is far away.

4

ELEANOR HAS A recurring dream. She is living single in an apartment with no children, and she hasn't had a date in ten years. In the dream, all of this is normal.

She has this dream in the very early hours of the morning, after an evening when her oldest son said to her, "All I want out of life is to have a day when you don't talk to me." This was after Eleanor had asked, "How was your day?"

She always asks this in the friendliest way that she can, half knowing that she is baiting Eugene, and half wanting to set a positive mood. Last night, Liam, his younger brother, said to him from the back seat of the car, "What do you want, to live alone the rest of your life?" Which seemed like a genuine question, not something to annoy his brother.

"Yes, that's what I want," Eugene answered.

"It's tough living alone, Eugene," Liam told him.

Eleanor supposed that for Eugene, living alone would mean that you did not have anyone to clean your room, to shop for your food, or to cook your meals. It meant, in essence, that life with home help was over. But Eleanor chose not to insert her opinions into this conversation. She suspected that Eugene would have a smart-ass answer to anything she said.

On the next evening, while putting out place settings at the kitchen island and taking dinner out of the oven, she muses that she never will have the life of her single-woman fantasy. She only has to look around to realize this.

Over homemade macaroni and cheese, Liam asks, "Is there anything else?"

Eleanor is standing on the opposite side of the island, which produces an unfortunate diner waitress effect. Frank, from the customer side, says generously to Liam, "Check the freezer for chicken nuggets." Chicken nuggets are *never* on Eleanor's shopping list. They are something Frank buys when he occasionally goes to the supermarket, on a weekend to help out, when he comes home with only processed frozen foods and fizzy drinks.

Eleanor breathes in deeply and counts to three. "No," she says to Liam. "They aren't on the menu tonight. You will eat what I've made for everyone." She knows that homemade macaroni and cheese is Eugene's favorite, and not Liam's. And that when Frank allows Liam to eat something else, there are leftovers that no one will want for lunch the next day, but not enough for a family meal. Frank always wants meat for lunch and the boys want peanut butter.

"Why?" Frank asks. "He has to eat something."

It's too much for Eleanor to explain her thoughts to him.

"I am not a short-order cook," she says, an irony from where she is standing, on the service side of the island. She puts down the spoon she has been holding and wipes her hands on her jeans before moving to the end of the island where her place is set. She is angry but trying to hold on to a calm mien in front of the boys.

Still, Frank continues as though he does not suspect the depth of his wife's anger. "Yogurt. Bagels. Scramble yourself some eggs." And then to Eleanor, "He won't ask you to make it for him. He'll do it for himself." Liam watches his father, then his mother, and says nothing. Eugene serves himself a second helping. Eleanor feels relieved that the leftover situation won't be as bad as she thought.

"That's not the point," she says to Frank. No. There was the extra trip to the supermarket, the effort put into making the dish and being there so that it comes out of the oven on time. She will clean the encrusted pan afterward, when the boys have scattered to do homework and Frank is nowhere to be found. She could have made it from a box, but she doesn't do that sort of thing. It is, however, the sort of thing Frank would do without a thought. She struggles to think of how to make her sons appreciate the difference.

Liam gets up from his chair before she can explain her point to him, before she can stop him, or convince his father more explicitly not to undermine her authority. Eleanor feels her defeat in the sound of the eggs Liam cracks with alarming skill. She feels left behind.

"It's not dinner, it's breakfast." He shrugs. "But I can take care of myself."

WHEN SHE LOOKS at her sons, Eleanor believes that she has only a small window into the workings of the male mind. As a young, dating woman, she imagined that she would eventually understand the behavior of men.

Later that evening, she is wakened by a knock at the bedroom door. A bird tweets as Eugene opens the door and creeps toward the bed. Eleanor swims toward full consciousness as Frank makes noises and rolls his back toward Eleanor and Eugene.

"I'm afraid I won't be able to get to sleep," Eugene says.

"What time is it?" Eleanor asks, even though, by the birds, she knows.

"Four o'clock."

"Just try."

"Do you have any better advice?" Eugene asks. "My girlfriend just broke up with me."

"I say you should go back to sleep," Frank says. "You will feel better tomorrow."

"She says there are warring factions in her brain."

Frank lets out a loud breath that must have begun from his gut and burst forth through his nose and mouth simultaneously. He sits up and puts on his glasses. "What are you talking about?"

Eugene picks up on Frank's harsh tone. "I'm not going to be able to sleep at all now. I'm sorry I woke you, Dad."

"What warring factions?" Frank asks.

"It's too long to explain," Eugene says. "Go back to sleep."

Frank turns to the digital clock radio at his side of the bed. "Have you been on the phone until now?"

"Sort of."

"And when did you begin this conversation?"

"A couple of hours ago."

"Jesus, Eugene, it's a school night." Frank emits another long-winded breath. "And before that?"

"We were texting."

Eleanor senses by the shadows in the dark that Eugene is shrugging his shoulders. She wants to hug him, but her body is so tired, and she doesn't think that a hug is what he wants. He is a talker. He wants someone to tell him what to do.

"I'm only seventeen," Eugene says quietly, almost as if he doesn't want them to hear. "How am I supposed to understand all of this?"

"You haven't really explained things," Frank says.

Eleanor wants to kick Frank under the blanket, knowing that he had no experience with girls at seventeen. She gives in to the instinct to hug her son. "Come here." He bends over, dutifully, and she reaches to kiss him on the forehead. "Go to bed. We can finish all of this in the morning." Eugene leaves. Frank turns onto his side. Eleanor listens to the hum of the ceiling fan and the tweets of the sparrows.

ELEANOR CAN'T HELP but be a little shocked at what Eugene tells her.

"She says she wants to try being a lesbian, that the two sides of her sexuality are fighting with each other," he says over his seven o'clock bowl of cereal. He is late. After brushing away the latest sparrow nesting material, Eleanor had knocked on his door to wake him, and was greeted with a muted "Fuck off!" She left him, only to return every ten minutes to try again. The disappointment she felt each time she heard him had crushed her. But now, minutes later, she experiences the revelation that she is needed again.

Yet, she can't tell if he is truly upset. His attention seems focused on food. He shovels cereal into his mouth, trying to accumulate as much as he can over his tongue and lower jaw, while at the same time he talks.

"I didn't realize . . . ," Eleanor says. "Maybe saying that is a way to let you down easily?" Looking at his expression, she is immediately sorry that she has said this. She is clearly an idiot. Eleanor asks instead, "What did you say to her?"

He looks up from his bowl. "This is not my fault," he says through the food in his mouth. "It just ended up that way. Why do you always have to talk these things out?"

"You woke me in the middle of the night to talk about it."

"I don't want to talk anymore." He swallows and waves his hand, his long narrow fingers splayed. "End of subject." He gets up from his bowl and glass and walks away to get ready for school.

Eleanor hears his brother, Liam, coming down the stairs. He is still in his pajama pants and T-shirt. Liam's middle school starts later than the high school. Without greeting his mother, he takes two eggs from the refrigerator, butter, and an English muffin, cracks the eggs and scrambles them in a soup bowl with a fork.

He looks up at his mother. "What was that? Was it about Margaret? They broke up, didn't they?"

"You're going to turn into an egg," Eleanor says.

There have been times when Eugene won't give Eleanor any information about the people he is texting with. So she asks Liam, who is three years younger, and doesn't fully understand his brother's acute need for privacy. Liam pays close attention to what his brother does, and Eugene, whom Eleanor believes is oblivious to things around him, is too focused on himself to notice.

Liam pours the eggs into a nonstick frying pan and uses a spatula to curdle them. The kitchen fills with the smell. "It was bound to happen," he says. "You don't have two-hour-long phone conversations without something really good or really bad happening."

Eleanor smiles at her younger son's youthful wisdom. "How do you know? You haven't had any girlfriends yet."

"I go on YouTube, Mom."

>‑<‑ →‑ →‑ →>‑<‑

WHEN THE HOUSE is finally empty, Eleanor sits in the kitchen, waiting for her computer to boot up, cradling the third mug of coffee in her palms. Annie barks at the back door because the recycling truck has pulled up in the alley behind the garage. Eleanor logs on to her Facebook account. Suddenly she isn't listening to the dog. Her head is light. She didn't expect an answer, not really. But there it is.

Hi Eleanor. Yes! I am the Phil Anderson from your high school trig class. Gosh that was a long time ago. And I haven't thought about math since then! Fun to hear from you! My oldest daughter goes to college in Evanston! How far from Northwestern are you? And guess what, I have a border collie. She is so smart she could be writing this message! I am about an hour and a half from you in a small town called Bailey. Good to hear you are so close. Tell me more about you, your family, and your dog. Sincerely, Phil.

For a moment, in her housewife morning, she has no children, she has no husband, and she is free. She can't hear extraneous noise, like nesting birds or the telephone ringing. Even if the sparrows are building their nasty little nests in the eaves of *her* house. She has a break in all of that. There is an opening before her. A clearing.

5

ELEANOR GETS KAYE'S call on Thursday morning: drinks at her house, she'll take care of everything. Eleanor senses that Kaye wants to get together more and more frequently, ever since Eric and Clara started work on the boat.

Eleanor changes from her T-shirt to a button-down blouse with small blue flowers and three-quarter sleeves. She applies mascara and lip gloss and walks to the happy hour. Kaye lives nearly a half mile from Eleanor's house, in an older neighborhood with straight streets that meet at perpendicular angles. The houses, most of them, were built between 1900 and 1930 and are largely well kept. Huge deciduous trees grow along the parkways and in the front lawns. During thunderstorms, branches break and fall in the grassy yards and across the sidewalks as evidence of their vulnerability.

It is mid-May and the petals of the first blooms lay scattered on the ground. Eleanor is cold without a jacket. In her bag she carries a bottle of decent red wine, something Frank's golfing partner brought with him when he invited himself to dinner. It had become a long dinner party. The golfing partner, newly separated from his wife, was morose. "We can't just ask him to leave," Frank had said, showing impressive empathy. Eleanor realized that the biggest surprise to her had been that she was married to a golfer, not that Frank wanted to take care of his friend, nor that he had unexpectedly brought home a dinner guest with emotional problems. Golf had not been a part of Frank's repertoire when they first met.

Three women are having cocktails at Kaye's this particular Thursday. Thursdays are good because they feel like the end of the week, but they don't get in the way of weekend family time.

Eleanor and Kaye met as room parents for their children's kindergarten class, where the school PTA created enough work to keep them busy. Both women took their responsibilities seriously, at least for that first year, hand making a papier-mâché solar system, creating all-inclusive winter holiday art and cooking projects, on-the-spot pancakes for the family breakfast, and the ever-stressful Teacher Appreciation Week breakfasts and lunches, where each grade took a day and each set of room parents prepared a meal for that day. This particular event had brought Eleanor and Kaye together for much-needed evening libations when the whole thing was over.

None of this was what Eleanor and Kaye had expected their lives to be when they were students and meeting their husbands. Eleanor had never had a full-time job that used her skills as a PhD candidate in English before getting pregnant and having children, only teaching assistantships and a brief part-time position at an open-enrollment college that paid her per class.

Now, Eleanor recognizes the cliché her life has become, with the constant barrage of popular fiction and television series. She feels her family has taken advantage of her as she drives her sons to music lessons, and cooks dinners that force her youngest son to make his own. She and her Thursday cocktail friends are always mildly annoyed at their husbands, who condescendingly tell them that they are high-maintenance women and laugh about it. "Why isn't there a reality TV show about *you*?" Because, Eleanor thinks, it would be dull.

Now all of the duties of room parents are long over. There are few rewards for her past volunteer work. Instead there is the achy feeling one gets when one's teenager berates one then instantly needs help afterward. Teenagers seem to need their mothers profoundly, in ways Eleanor and her friends would not have imagined, to talk to at odd times about homework, or teen love, or to tell Mom that she sucks at parenting.

For only a brief time, Eleanor, encouraged by her friends, thought about going back to school to finish her PhD, but all of the people she had originally worked with were either retired or dead. And her research had not been significant. Kaye once wanted Eleanor to partner with her to write grant proposals for nonprofits, but then the economy dipped.

Some days Eleanor feels that she could burst from the tedium. There are things Eleanor wants to say to her friends, she considers, as she approaches Kaye's house. That she is bored during the day, even when she is very busy doing something voluntary and useful. When surrounded by people, she still feels alone. She is frightened that she will have to fill her time when her sons go off to college in a few years.

Maybe she could be reckless and not worry about consequences, skip her vitamins for a week, stay up late one or two nights without worrying about having to wake up early, or fall asleep naturally without having her anxieties take over.

Exchange emails with Phil Anderson without worrying about how far it could go, or what he was really thinking. She wants to be able to drive without a seat belt. She wants to go fast.

KAYE'S HOUSE IS vast and lined in dark oak, as an original Arts and Crafts home might be, but Eleanor knows that Kaye has had it meticulously remodeled to look this way. The kitchen is painted a dark blue with oak cabinets and wrought iron handles. The three women sit on benches around an antique wood table.

Kaye has provided a beautiful arrangement of multicolored tortilla chips with various dips from a Central Street caterer. They drink wine from thick sturdy glasses that were a wedding gift from a longtime friend of Eric's.

They talk about Eleanor's upcoming thirtieth high school reunion. "Remember when I thought you should bring me as your lesbian lover for your twenty-fifth?" Kaye says.

Eleanor shakes her head. "Could we not go there?"

Their other friend Magda smiles as she holds a chip overwhelmed with salsa, and pulls a straight brown hair out from where it is caught in the corner of her mouth.

"Going as a lesbian couple only shocks if people care," Eleanor says. "We aren't lesbians, we aren't a couple, and no one I went to high school with cares."

"I think you look young for your age," Magda says, moving her eyes along Eleanor's face as though she is looking for lines.

"She's forty-eight," Kaye says. "How old are you?"

"Forty-five."

"I'm sure that compared to the other folks at the reunion, Eleanor will look good. Everyone else there has, I'm sure, put on a ton of weight, and people in our neighborhood work out and we diet like there's no tomorrow. I doubt they do that in every community. So, she will have that. Eleanor, you have distinguished yourself by aging well. You should go. Even if they have no idea who you are. They will look at you and want to know you."

"They certainly did *not* want to know me when I was sixteen."

"Don't go as a lesbian," Magda says. "And don't talk to them about being a liberal."

"No one is going to care if you are a liberal now, they only care about high school," Kaye says. "Is there someone you want to see?"

Like Phil, Eleanor's new pen pal? Who, during the past week, in emails, has written that he lives only an hour and a half away and that his daughter goes to Northwestern, not far from Eleanor's house? And sometimes he comes into town, and would they ever run into each other?

Eleanor has the geek girl fantasy of showing up to a high school reunion on the arm of a beautiful former football player. But she doesn't even know for sure what Phil looks like now.

PHIL'S EMAILS ARE upbeat with an undertone of vulnerability that leads Eleanor to think that he is confiding in her. A part of her wonders why and a part of her enjoys the attention, the second part being more dominant. He asks more about her day than her husband, Frank, does. But mostly, he wants her opinion. He doesn't seem to talk at her. They are writing to each other; it is a discussion, an exchange.

This is what she thinks about while she is sitting with her friends, in a haze of alcohol.

Sometimes I get an email from you and it's the bright spot of my day of boring work with the almost-ex-wife. At night we have to sit at the dining room table with each other and divide up all our crap, even our kids' time. So, tell me, what are you up to today? Are you meeting your friends for coffee? Are you walking your dog? Are you cooking something interesting?

Magda and Kaye absorb themselves in a complicated story while Eleanor pretends to listen. She stares out the window above the sink, watching the branches and leaves move in the light. Phil writes to her long emails that interest her, and always end with an open question, and an expectation that she will answer. While he frequently writes early in the morning, she tries to wait until later in the afternoon to answer him, so that she doesn't appear anxious or too solicitous. She is married. She isn't sure where he is going with this.

His wife is leaving him, but she hasn't *actually* left yet. She still lives in the house. He says that he is the one taking care of the daughter who is still in high school, though she is rarely home. He cooks the evening meals and does most of the housekeeping. It's going to be his house. His wife spends a lot of time "out there" looking for a new place to live. Eleanor suspects that Phil's wife has found someone new. Or at least, wants to find someone new. After twenty years of marriage, you wonder what is on the other side, just as the beauty of your body and hair begin to fade.

Eleanor thinks of all of this when she reads Phil's emails (all four of them). She has not seen him in twenty-five years. She knew him in high school, lost touch with him during college, and wondered what happened to him. He had joined the marines at some point. She'd wondered if he had seen combat. During that time, she'd asked other people about him, but no one knew anything. Of all things, Eleanor had not imagined him married.

Sitting at Kaye's kitchen table amidst the buzz of the other women's voices, Eleanor wonders: What if I wasn't bored at home? What if Frank made surprise dinner reservations every month or so? What if he laughed at my jokes? What if he made his kids eat the dinner she had prepared every night? Would I still be interested in connecting with Phil?

So, Phil writes to Eleanor. He emails photos of his daughter and her junior prom date. He talks about his vegetable garden. She counters by asking him if it isn't too early for lettuce (she has a black thumb). Phil says that he saves Eleanor's emails in a file because they make him laugh.

So, what does Eleanor do about this at the cocktail hour with Kaye and Magda? As she sits there and lets the wine slip from her lips to her brain, eating, smiling as though she is really listening. She is far away wondering what Phil is doing right now. Is he watching his younger daughter at an athletic event? Is he still trying to have family dinners? Is he reading, listening to music, doing anything Eleanor would find interesting? Is he dreaming about his wife?

Early in Frank's career, when trading firms had big holiday parties and everyone dressed to the nines to go, Eleanor learned that she could nod and smile and half listen to conversations that didn't hold her interest. So, she is not listening to Sheryl Crow piped into the kitchen, or to much of what her friends are discussing. Her mind is a million miles away: there are imaginary hands on her shoulders, there is imaginary breath in her ear.

Eleanor, This thing with Linda has been dragging out—the "her living here in the house" thing. She goes out on weekend nights like she is a teenager. She doesn't even talk to me unless it's about the furniture. Eleanor, what would you do in this situation? What would you do?

AS ELEANOR THINKS of Phil's emails, Kaye opens the third bottle. Eleanor can't believe they've got this far. It is clear that Magda is tipsy. She teaches at the university, and in her department, a young, unbalanced woman has filed a sexual harassment suit against a male professor, who is Magda's office mate. It is the student's word against her office mate's and there are clearly subtleties and lies on both parts. "Although," Magda says, holding her index finger in the air, "These things are never cut-and-dried." She pushes her glass toward Kaye for a refill. She has been telling a long story. It is now impossible for her to be in her office with this man. When Eleanor wakes up from her daydream to pay attention to Magda, she realizes it's a story she's heard before.

Eleanor wishes she could unload her own thoughts as Magda has done, to talk about the emails from Phil, but it's too risky. "You're getting loopy," she tells Magda.

"Kaye keeps filling my glass."

Kaye rolls her eyes as she pours.

"You're going to have to leave your car here and walk home," Eleanor says to Magda.

"It isn't far. I can walk."

"You're a safe drunk," Kaye tells her.

Magda frowns and changes the subject. "How is the boat going, Kaye?"

"It's complicated. There were Vikings in Scotland. And yet, one does not have to be a Viking, or even Scottish, to want to build a Viking boat."

"How do you build it?" Eleanor realizes she has never asked for the details.

"From a kit," Kaye says. "One day a large truck pulls up in the alleyway of your house and men unload a Viking boat kit. Wood. Directions. You can buy a prefab vacation house and have it sent in a kit from Scandinavia. So, why not a boat?"

"It's like an Ikea boat," Magda says.

"You should both come and see it sometime."

Kaye turns toward one of the walls, then she turns back again. "I have a picture of the finished product somewhere. I'm not in the mood to get it out. This is their thing. Eric and Clara's. I stay out of it. I don't know a thing about boats. I have a recurring nightmare of taking the stupid thing out into the harbor and everyone pointing and laughing as we try to set sail in it as a family. It's like that dream you have where you arrive at school without your clothes and there is no way you can go home to get them. The only thing that would save me would be for it to sink in shallow water and it not to be my fault."

Magda and Eleanor stare at Kaye without saying anything. Magda puts down the tortilla chip that was heading for her mouth and says, "You could always pretend that you are part of someone else's family."

"Anybody else's," Eleanor says. Then they sit there for a moment, relishing their unhappiness, almost seeking comfort in it.

KAYE EMERGES FROM her house in the dim light and opens the passenger door to Eleanor's car. "Just drive," she says.

Kaye doesn't explain, and Eleanor knows not to ask. The teenage boys in the next yard look up at the sound of the car door shutting. They are tall and lean young men, pushing each other on the neighbor's front lawn, boys who three years ago refused to interact with Eugene in middle school. Eleanor is sure they would not recognize her or her car because these aren't things that teenage boys pay attention to, so her disapproval of them means nothing.

Eleanor has left Frank at home watching the NBA finals, while her sons sit in front of their computers. She and Kaye are meeting Phil Anderson at a music club near the university, where his daughter is entered in a band contest. The phone call surprised Eleanor. "What are you and Frank doing tonight?" Phil had said. "I'm coming into town."

Eleanor made sure that Frank would be busy before she invited Kaye. The invitation did not seem for a couple. "An old friend from high school. But the playoffs are tonight, aren't they?" It hadn't been difficult.

They drive toward the quaint downtown. Kaye assumes a directing role, even though it isn't her gig, and Eleanor thinks to herself that she doesn't need this behavior. They turn on to a residential street that runs into the lakeshore to the east, and pass the YMCA building, tall, lit up, taking up an entire block. Along the tree-lined street that runs under the el tracks, they park, and Eleanor feeds the meter with all the quarters they have. They walk under the bridge and around the corner to the club.

Kaye is muttering and Eleanor isn't paying attention. She can feel the blood pumping in her neck. They pick a table outside on the front sidewalk patio of the club and wait for a waitress. Kaye says that she is thirsty; Eleanor has a dry mouth. There is a line of college-aged kids at the front door of the club, just beyond their table.

After twenty minutes of quietly sipping beer, Eleanor notes that Kaye is in a better mood. "Is that *him*? The aging Nordic god walking our way?" Kaye says.

To Eleanor, the comment isn't a compliment. Phil is tall and well built, and his blond hair is spiked in a hairstyle that, to Eleanor, seems too youthful. Yet, she is impressed that he has cleaned up to meet her. He wears a black leather jacket, though it is really too warm for it. He grins as he arrives at their table, and Kaye and Eleanor stand. While Eleanor considers whether to shake his hand, he grabs her arm and abruptly kisses her cheek. The action is so swift and jarring that her face goes hot, and for a moment she thinks she has stopped breathing. She introduces Phil to Kaye, who stares blankly at him before taking his hand. Eleanor interprets this as Kaye's way of saying, "Is this it?" and she feels exposed.

They show their driver's licenses to the bouncer, who

must be twenty-one but doesn't look it. He is the size of a football player, and gives them each a wristband that, as Kaye remarks, does little to hide the fact that they are old enough to be everyone else's parents. Phil pays for the three of them before Eleanor can reach into her pocket for her cash.

Inside the club, the room is hot, loud, and dark, and smells of spilled beer, Mr. Clean, and sweat. She can feel perspiration gather at the back of her neck and under her hair, but she sees that, as Phil looks at the mass of moving people, he doesn't remove his leather jacket.

Eleanor feels as if she is in a mosh pit, though it is difficult to remember what that was like. All around them, white undergraduates sway, wave, and call out to the band on the small stage in the front of the room. The boys wear faded baseball caps worn backwards and molded to their heads, the girls are in tight jeans and ballet flats.

Phil smiles at Kaye and Eleanor, and points with his head. "She's in the crowd," he says.

"Who?" Eleanor assumes he is talking about his daughter.

"My almost-ex."

Kaye leans toward Eleanor's ear. "Who?"

"His daughter's mother," Eleanor says. "His wife."

The current band finishes and they can now hear each other talk. Eleanor asks Phil to point out his wife, Linda. He does so. She is with another, older woman, at the opposite side of the crowded room. Phil tells her that the older woman is Linda's mother. Linda Anderson is taller than Eleanor had expected, blonde and thin. She doesn't seem aware that Phil is in the room, or that Eleanor and Kaye are watching her.

The next band sets up and Eleanor recognizes Jilly, Phil's older daughter, from a YouTube video of a pop song cover.

She bends over to adjust a microphone stand and her blonde roller curls fall over her face and shoulders.

Jilly wears prim shoes, the kind of pumps she might have borrowed from her grandmother. She doesn't fit in with the saggy-pants boys around her who are setting up the drum kit and adjusting the amplifiers. Phil leans down to Eleanor and explains that his daughter's music is "folkie." The type you might wear old lady shoes to listen to, Eleanor thinks. "This doesn't feel like her crowd," Phil says.

Jilly plays for about twenty minutes, and no one in the audience seems to be paying attention, except for Eleanor, Phil, and Kaye, as well as the almost-ex and her mother. They watch Jilly's lips move, they hear the bass and drums, but Eleanor has trouble hearing Jilly. Her voice is soft and, as she sways and flips her hair, the ruckus around her drowns it out. Phil's face is sunken. When she finishes playing, he says that he needs to help Jilly take down and disappears. He will meet Eleanor and Kaye outside.

In the artificial yellow light on the sidewalk of the club, Kaye looks sour. "That was painful," she says to Eleanor. "What do we do now?"

What are they supposed to do now, go home? Eleanor digs in her heels and turns her head to look for Phil's wife and mother-in-law. They are both standing nearby. Even in the dim light, Eleanor can see that Linda is not a natural blonde, and that her clothes hang on her thin body. She puts out her hand to Linda. "I'm Eleanor," she says. "I went to high school with Phil. I live around here."

"Hi," she says. "I'm Linda." Near her, Eleanor feels short and sloppy. She looks to the mother-in-law, but Linda doesn't offer up her name.

"We enjoyed hearing your daughter sing," Eleanor says. She can feel the tension in the air like the humidity, thick and unforgiving.

"Thank you," Linda says. She plays with a strand of her hair, curling it around her fingers in a childish act that doesn't match the sternness of her voice. "Where is it you live?"

Eleanor points behind her. "That way."

"Away from the lake? I like the beach."

Eleanor nods.

Phil finally emerges from the club, pausing outside the door before clapping his hands together and looking in the direction of Linda and Eleanor. "Have you all met yet?" he asks them. It's Kaye who answers, "Yes," abruptly so that they don't have to go through introductions again. Phil looks at Eleanor then Kaye, then back to Eleanor again. "Then let's eat!" He is ebullient.

They follow Phil into the bar and grill next door to the club. As they enter, the waiter says that they are closing the restaurant, so only the bar menu is available. This doesn't faze Phil, but Eleanor is not sure if she and Kaye should stay. Kaye looks hungry, rolling her eyes as the waiter makes his announcement. She is always hungry, and perhaps feeding her is better than taking her home. "I need another drink," Kaye says.

They are led through the dark, half-full bar to a table, and as they walk in the dim light, Eleanor can see the boy Phil once was beneath his windburned cheeks and whitening blond hair. She thinks that it is thoughtful of him to help his mother-in-law to her chair. The mother-in-law sits silently and watches Eleanor and Kaye.

Eleanor feels the urge to say, "So, here we are," but

doesn't. Then Phil and his wife exchange mutterings about the journey to town. The waiter takes drink orders and is mercifully fast in delivering them. Linda turns her wine at the base of the glass with thin manicured fingers. The nails, varnished in a natural pink, shine as if the paint is new. She doesn't pick up the glass. Eleanor sips her own beer. Kaye downs half of her Blue Moon and sucks on the orange rind. Phil smiles as if he is not aware of the strangeness. His mood invigorates Eleanor. It's positive.

Kaye takes the orange rind out of her mouth. "So how long has your daughter been singing?"

The almost-ex defers to Phil in an obviously well-rehearsed act, by turning her chin and looking up at him under her domed eyelids. Phil shrugs uncomfortably. "Piano lessons, maybe in first grade? She sang at church and at school. I don't know. She put a band together senior year of high school?"

Linda nods. *He's passed her test,* Eleanor thinks, and wonders if now they will act like a couple.

"Very talented," Kaye says of Phil's daughter.

Eleanor plays with the tiny diamond pendant around her neck. Linda watches her. "Nice necklace," she says.

"Present from my husband," Eleanor says. Eleanor doesn't want Linda to think that she is chasing Phil. She also wants to understand what sort of uncomfortable game Phil and Linda are playing.

There is no way to leave now that they have ordered food.

Kaye spreads her lips suspiciously and starts on her next Blue Moon. The food arrives. Phil looks at the avocado half on top of Kaye's salad, and as though he were marking his territory, he smiles coyly, "I love avocados." He winks at Eleanor, and Kaye takes him seriously, picking up the avocado with her fingertips and dropping it in the middle of Phil's plate. "I hate them," Kaye says. Linda raises her eyebrows. *Does she think he is flirting with her?* Eleanor wonders. *Is he?*

Linda turns her glass and smiles periodically. She pokes at her food with a fork. Eleanor suspects that Linda thinks Kaye is funny—everyone does—but isn't letting on. Linda arranges her food into four neat piles on her plate, which must be, Eleanor thinks, the secret to her narrow figure. She notices that Linda does not bite, chew or swallow, she just plays with her food, and she recalls how Phil has said what an excellent cook Linda is.

Linda turns to Kaye, "What do you do?"

Kaye raises her head from her beer, not expecting the question. She smiles. "I'm a police detective."

Eleanor looks at Kaye, but Kaye doesn't look back. Then Eleanor feels Kaye's foot on top of hers, pressing down until Eleanor is forced to gasp because it hurts. Kaye is wearing cowboy boots and the heel is hard on Eleanor's sandaled instep. She closes her watering eyes.

The almost-ex raises her eyebrows and tosses her blonde hair. It's the hair Eleanor dreamed of having in high school, long and straight. "That's an interesting profession," Linda says. "What do you do as a detective?"

Kaye smiles slyly. Eleanor turns her body so that her feet are not near Kaye's. "Drugs, gambling. Vice."

Eleanor realizes that she is holding tightly onto her glass.

"We just broke up an illegal poker club. Something called Cobra's in the South Loop," Kaye says.

Linda seems interested. She nods and smiles and looks genuine, to Eleanor. Phil appears not to know how to enter the conversation. All of this encourages Kaye to keep going.

"They didn't see it coming."

Eleanor considers all of the reality crime shows Kaye watches when she is at home, bored, waiting for her daughter to return with the car, or her husband to emerge from the garage, and she wishes Kaye would take up a hobby, like knitting. Then Phil smiles at Eleanor, and she sees there is nothing she can do. He is enjoying himself, or he is acting as if he is. She wants him to enjoy himself, to enjoy having met her, even if the situation is deadly uncomfortable. Eleanor had imagined she'd have some time to catch up with Phil, the three of them, her, and Kaye, and Phil, at a small table drinking wine and laughing. Kaye would be there to make sure it was all legit. And Phil might send Eleanor a signal that he is interested in her and give her the chance to step out of her boring life, to play with fire. But that scenario is clearly not happening.

"Flak jackets, big guns, battering ram. The whole nine yards," Kaye says. "We took in ten people."

"No kidding," Linda says. She takes a sip from her wine glass. "You broke down the door?"

Linda is getting comfortable. She is drinking. Clearly, she and Kaye watch the same shows.

"Actually, with all of that equipment, the uniforms rang the doorbell and a guy answered."

Uniforms?

"Was the club hidden?" the almost-ex asks.

"Storefront. Not hidden at all."

This is Kaye's way of making it seem real.

"They didn't post a neon sign saying they were gambling illegally, if that's what you mean," Kaye says.

Then, Phil asks, "How long have you been doing this, Kaye?"

Does he suspect?

Kaye shrugs and drinks. "About fifteen years." Then she excuses herself, smiling, and on the way to the ladies' she stops the waiter and orders another beer.

Eleanor looks at Phil and says that she will be right back. In the twenty steps to the toilet, she struggles to understand why Phil and Linda are playing along, or if they could even believe Kaye's story. Maybe it's because they are unfamiliar with Kaye and they know no police officers. Eleanor is furious. Kaye has upstaged her big meeting with Phil. The ladies' room door slams behind her, and the words, "I can't believe you are lying like this!" come rushing out of her mouth. A young mother with a toddler looks at her with wide, open eyes and shields her son as they exit. "He's up rather late," Eleanor says, hoping that they have heard.

"I'm taking a piss in here," Kaye says from behind the toilet stall door.

Eleanor stands in front of Kaye's stall and realizes that this entire evening is a disaster. She wants someone to blame, but there is no specific event that points her toward that person, just one element after another. Kaye is Kaye and she has had too much to drink. Phil is Phil—perhaps not wanting to exclude anyone, even the wife he is divorcing. After all, they are here for their daughter, though that was not made clear to Eleanor in the invitation. Thank goodness she had the presence of mind to bring her own chaperone (there was never any question in her mind of bringing Frank). All of this leaves Eleanor feeling like the uncomfortable interloper. She will have to revisit this whole thing.

Kaye is going to ignore Eleanor's complaints, so Eleanor leaves the ladies' room and returns to the table. Eventually,

Kaye follows.

Eleanor is now ready to leave, and there is an ache inside of her as she waits anxiously to announce that she and Kaye must go. Then the waiter brings Linda another glass of wine. Eleanor wonders what happened to the first one.

"Camping in the desert—" Phil begins and Linda finishes, "—Is no place for ladies? Is that what you wanted to say?" she asks Phil. Eleanor has missed a part of the conversation. *Please tell me Kaye didn't also say that she was in the military,* Eleanor thinks. Then, "It was the first Gulf War. I don't really remember details," Phil says. But how could you forget that? Eleanor wonders. It must be that he doesn't want to talk about something his wife brought up.

Kaye pulls out her iPhone as she finishes her beer. The evening is done. Eleanor can finally say that they need to go.

FRANK IS ASLEEP when Eleanor comes home. He has left his bedside lamp on so that she can see her way through to the bed.

Eleanor can see this from the top of the stairs and the hallway. In his own room, Eugene sits on his bed with a handheld game console and the bedroom door wide open. He looks up and waves to his mother. Liam's door is closed, and from the crack beneath it, Eleanor sees that his light is off.

Frank is on top of the bedcover with his pajamas on, still wearing his eyeglasses. The television is on with the volume low, and periodically he sputters a gasping snore. Eleanor remembers that once she found this charming. She removes his glasses and sets them on the pile of books on his bedside table. She turns off the television and the lamp and waits for her eyes to adjust to the dark. When she finally crawls into bed, she finds that Frank's skin is warm and damp. In his unconsciousness he shakes her off and then turns on his side, away from her.

She rolls to the other side of the bed. She looks up at the ceiling and the shadows cast by the fan. The birds are gone now. It's too late for them. She is energized by the evening, disappointed, wondering if she should try to see Phil again or just drop it. Did she make a mistake in staying to go to the restaurant? Was the point of the invitation really just to hear his daughter, or was it to see Phil? Did she get all of this wrong? Then, again, the wife and her mother arrived separately.

She picks up her phone and there is a brief text from Phil. "I'm sorry about tonight. Didn't expect my wife and her mother. They weren't planning to come. Enjoyed meeting your friend. Hope you aren't upset."

She starts to type. It can't hurt, she thinks. "The birds are quiet now," she writes. "It was an interesting evening. I hope you got home ok."

It's all she can think of to say to him as her brain flutters with information and she tries to get to sleep.

7

PHIL LEAVES THE restaurant and watches Eleanor and Kaye walk under the el tracks. A fog is settling, the streets are wet, and he can hear their heels click on the pavement. Their voices fade with the growing distance, through the increasingly dense air and the crevices between buildings. A train passes over the bridge. Phil feels the ground vibrate, and the sky around him lights up in a flash. Then it is gone and the air is quiet. He is startled at the longing he has as he watches Eleanor go. The whole thing was his idea, and he knew that he could have met her and felt nothing. It is all up to chemistry. He knows that. And then his almost-ex decided to appear with her mother. Everyone had seemed to act on their best behavior. And, he had explained to Linda that this was just a meeting, a renewing of an old friendship. He waits until he can no longer see Eleanor's body fade ahead of him, along with her friend's.

His family is gathering in Jilly's apartment, and his daughter has asked him to come. It is late and he is tired and trying to work off the beer he has just had. It usually doesn't affect him, because he is a big guy. He won't drive home if he feels tipsy, and it is an hour and a half to his house from here. He

3

walks quickly along the empty street and beneath the awnings on Chicago Avenue. There are no other people walking, and few cars. It seems silly to wait at the light to cross the street, but he does. These late-night gatherings have become more awkward with the deterioration of his marriage, and the way he and Linda arrive and leave separately. He feels that he has to try to be there if he wants to be in his daughter's life.

Jilly lives on a small street off of a main avenue, about a ten-minute walk from the club where she sang. He enters through a glass-fronted door. Her small apartment is wedged between two storefront businesses in an old, multilevel, white brick building with 1919 carved into the cornerstone. He rings the buzzer next to her name and enters the second glass door. He climbs the steps two at a time, and he can hear the muffled voices of the young men in the band as he approaches the apartment. The door is ajar. He walks through it and sees his daughter smile.

The rest of the group looks up. His mother-in-law is seated in an easy chair, the only one in the studio. His wife is on the edge of a low futon bed. His daughter and the three boys in her band are sprawled on the floor. He already sees that this will be physically uncomfortable for him.

"Where have you been?" his wife asks.

He smiles. He wants to keep the atmosphere friendly. He sees this as his job now that his wife has decided to leave him. It might make things easier for Jilly. "Just seeing off the gals. Not a big deal," he says.

He steps over the college boys in the band. He wants to tell Linda that she shouldn't call attention to everything he does, but instead he closes his eyes for a small moment of peace. "Great concert, hon," he tells his daughter, reaching to kiss her on her cheek. It pains him to lie to her.

"There's Diet Coke and beer in the fridge, Dad," his daughter says. He takes a can of soda from the refrigerator in the corner kitchenette. With that in his fist, he leans against the wall and drinks, staring down at the young people on the floor, his wife primly seated with her back straight on the bed, his mother-in-law beginning to doze in her chair, her head flopped against its upholstered side. She snores softly, and the boys from the band snicker. "Grandma's making noise," one of them says.

From where Phil has stationed himself, he can sense how out of place he is. His wife projects tension, the way her face is alert and the way she sits, upright, her legs crossed at the ankles. She doesn't meet his eyes—she won't—and yet he thinks she knows he is waiting for her to acknowledge him with a glance. *Give me a break,* he thinks to himself. *You don't want to stay married, what am I supposed to do? Every woman I talk to now, like Eleanor, or even look at, you scrutinize, like she is a potential mistress.*

He focuses on his daughter. "What did you think of the concert?" he asks her.

From the floor, her legs to her side, she looks at her knees, taking on a protective posture Phil has seen many times before when she is insecure, curling into herself. "I don't even think anyone could hear us," she says.

Someone in the band grunts, "They were drunk. They didn't care."

"Wish we were," another of the band members says.

Phil wants to comfort his daughter as he did when she was younger. Though now he is almost embarrassed to touch her with his wife there. "I'm sure they could hear you," he says.

Again, he isn't telling the truth. She tilts her head to one side, then downward, and he remembers her as a child, her small pink cheeks beneath the sun hat. When, at that age, she was sad, she would contort her face and he would see her brown eyes flood with tears. Then, he was able to comfort her by picking her up and holding her. He could stop the crying by lifting up the little sundress covering her white belly and pressing his lips to just below her rib cage, blowing a loud, ticklish raspberry. Now, there is nothing he can do, especially with his wife and mother-in-law present. He wants to reach over to touch Jilly's shoulder, but it is complicated now, more complicated than it was when he could soothe her without words.

"There will be other concerts, right?" he says. *Always be optimistic,* he wants to tell her. Or even, *It will be fine in the morning.* But he knows that she is too smart for that. So, he drinks his soda and watches.

Funny how he used to be able to comfort her mother, too, with words and gestures, taking her by her shoulders and talking in her ear so that she could feel the tickle of his breath. Now, she is so thin and bony. He wonders what would happen if he touched her. She seems to have stopped eating since they began to divorce.

A boy from the band chuckles. He is lounging on his side, propping up his torso with his elbow and stretching his legs out between bodies and pieces of furniture. He doesn't look optimistic. "Other concerts," he says, and tips back his beer. Jilly is sulking, which is something that Phil knows comes to her naturally. She has always been dramatic. The three band members don't seem to notice this, or even care, and if they share her disappointment, it isn't obvious.

"I'd better get going," Phil says. "Lots to do tomorrow." He wants to leave before his daughter tires of him, but he doesn't know when that will be. These kids never sleep. He doesn't know how long Linda will stay. She always stays longer than he does, longer than she should. Perhaps because she needs Jilly more than he does, more than Jilly needs her. But Phil can't tell her this.

He really does have things to do tomorrow. He needs to clean the house, weed his vegetable garden, mow the lawn. He leaves his soda can near the sink and reaches over to kiss his daughter again. She looks up to him and says, "You could come to the concert *with* Mom next time. You could come together."

"You know how it is, Jilly."

"Next time just come *with* her."

How can he say no? "I'll try." He pats his mother-in-law on the shoulder and she stirs in her sleep. His wife even tries on a flat smile as he says, "Bye, everyone," and opens the door, and walks away.

On the drive home, he tries to keep his mind blank. He sees excerpts of scenes from the evening, his daughter on stage, his wife's cool looks, her interest in Eleanor's friend, and, of course, Eleanor herself. And then there is Jilly, "You could come together." Do children ever agree that their parents should split? How much does Jilly know of his marriage? The cheating, the man Linda is seeing, the church, what does she really know? Does this mean his daughter doesn't love him?

West of the city lights he continues past clusters of warehouses, junkyards, then glass office parks lit up as if they will launch, and newly planted farms to the side of the road beyond all of that. His mind is overloaded. He feels it between his eyes and in the pit of his stomach. He is tired. His neck hurts. He puts the Rolling Stones into the CD player because that is what he has, but he doesn't really listen to it.

At home, he puts his phone on the table near the front door. He lets the dog out and checks her water bowl. His younger daughter is asleep in her room; he can see her hair splayed above her blanket through the crack left in the partially closed door. He goes to the bathroom attached to his own bedroom, brushes and flosses his teeth. He lets go a heavy stream of urine into the toilet and washes his face and hands. He removes his clothes and crawls under his blanket thinking of how his body and head ache with fatigue. Downstairs his phone receives a message from Eleanor. But she is far away now. He turns his light off, feels a clenching in the back of his throat as if he holds in a sob, and he holds his breath for a while until the feeling dissipates. Then he lies there, waiting for sleep.

THE VEGETABLE GARDEN is hot under the early sun, and the low stalks tickle his bare feet and ankles. He bends over to remove the weeds, step-by-step, along the space between the rows. Phoenix barks, running and stopping to bury her nose in the grass. By the time Phil looks up to see that a small rabbit has appeared, Phoenix is on it, ears pricked, mouth open, but then the rabbit is gone, beneath the evergreen bushes that mark his property from the next-door neighbor's. Phoenix barks again.

Phil's youngest daughter is not yet awake. He'd like to

make her breakfast one of these days, just as he used to do on weekends before his wife decided to leave him. But she sleeps so late that it's lunchtime by the time she emerges. Phil's wife has already left the house. He knows because her bedroom door is open, and her car is missing from the garage. Where would she be after coming home in the early hours of morning? Did she sleep? Has she eaten breakfast? Is she attending the Saturday church service?

He must have drifted into sleep and not heard her come home. Eventually, he woke when the sun peered through the narrow spaces between the curtain panels, but he does not feel rested. Lately, he has not slept deeply or for long. He keeps books by the bed to read when he wakes up in the middle of the night; sometimes they distract him from the personal thoughts that keep him awake. Eleanor has recommended some titles to him. Phil enjoys reading, but it is like listening to music, he wants to hear what he is in the mood to hear, and sometimes Eleanor's choices don't interest him. Yet, he wants to try. He wants to please her, and he wants her to sympathize with him, to think he is a good person.

After an hour outside, the sun is quite strong. Phoenix is lying in the cool grass on her side. She senses that Phil is watching her and pops her head up, uttering a low, growling sigh. Then she puts her head down again. All this makes Phil smile.

Soon, when he can feel the sweat on his neck trickle down his back, he goes inside to the kitchen to make some coffee. While it is brewing, he opens his laptop and checks his email. There is a brief message from Eleanor about the night before. "All quiet here," he writes back. "I enjoyed seeing you, too. How can we see each other again?" He adds that he would like to meet her family as well, but also have the private conversation they weren't able to have this last time, to catch up. In past emails she has hinted at inviting him for an evening or even a weekend. "We aren't far from the lake and we could all go to the beach." Does she mean herself, her husband, and Phil, too? "Or have a cookout," she had written. Would it be a break from the stress and dead quiet of his home? Would it put her out too much?

The clock in the family room chimes nine times. Phil warms the shower water upstairs, goes to his closet and retrieves khaki shorts and a neatly folded navy blue T-shirt. He showers and dresses. He shaves. He sees again, out the window, that the day will be clear.

His daughter is still not awake. And where is Linda? Is she with the younger man? If he goes to church and stands in the wings again, will he see her? By the window, he takes the drapes in his hand and considers a quick drive to church.

Years ago, when they were unhappy, and she decided not to sleep with him anymore, he found another woman. And they lived distant lives.

Now he is helpless. He feels the tension in the back of his throat, the ache in his head, behind his eyes, and he takes a deep breath to suppress the sob. He pinches the bridge of his nose until it goes away. He is alone, but he does not want to be emotional, not even if there is no one to see it. So, he looks out at the front yard, the neighbor's Japanese maple tree, deep red against the yellow brick of the front of the house, the curves of the branches as they dip toward the grass. It is windless and the sun reflects off the street, bright and moving toward midday, its apex, as he watches.

8

CLARA MAKES AN angry face as she peers down on her mother's sleeping head. "You wore my cowboy boots," she says.

She watches as Kaye rolls from her side to her back, then opens her eyes and looks up, but doesn't say anything. Maybe she can't, Clara thinks. Maybe she has a hangover. It would not be surprising. "Mother," she says. "They smell like beer. They are caked with mud."

"How do you know what beer smells like?" Her mother's voice is muffled by the blanket.

"I bought those boots with my own money." To Clara, answering a question from a drunk about how you know about the smell of beer seems stupid.

"They were at the front door. I was in a hurry."

"Mother!"

"Until you leave my house, presumably for college, everything that you think is yours is really mine, by virtue of the fact that it is in *my* house."

"But I used my babysitting money to pay for them. They're three-hundred-dollar boots."

"No one your age should be wearing boots that cost that much."

Clara looks down at Kaye's red face. Clara thinks her mother might throw up. So, she leaves, decisively communicating her anger with each weighty footfall.

Clara lies on the plump down comforter that covers her bed. She had cleaned her room earlier looking for some of her homework. She takes her phone from next to the clock and texts Jenny. "Are you home? I need to get out. My mom's an asshole." It is stupid to stay here. Her father is out. Her mother is hung over. Her boots are destroyed.

How *could* she have destroyed them!

Clara takes her phone, her house keys, and puts on a pair of flip-flops. She is out the door in thirty seconds.

THE HANGOVER IS all Eleanor's fault, for bringing Kaye to an event where she could only maintain her interest by drinking beer. Kaye hiccups bile. She imagines Eric, her own husband, trying to play the part of the Norse god someday, with the same ineptness as that guy Phil had. But for Kaye it would be different. If Eric had an old flame, an Eleanor, she would be in Scotland. They would have to go all the way to Scotland to repeat the scenario.

Then Kaye remembers pretending to be a police detective.

As she opens her closet looking for a sweater to cover her nightgown, she thinks of how sometimes, when you don't feel well, it doesn't bother you that you may have acted ridiculous the night before. She spots the packed overnight bag in the corner, something she prepared on a particularly bad night with her husband and daughter. She hasn't yet unpacked it, and it seems a silly fight over cowboy boots isn't a reason for her to leave. But the suitcase is there. And it makes her feel better.

Downstairs she fills the coffee maker for the second run of coffee. Eric seems to have finished the first pot. She doesn't hear him in the house, but that is normal. He moves in a stealthy way, surprising her when she isn't ready for a surprise. It is an intensely annoying habit. Mercifully, he hasn't done it this morning.

The coffee is bitter and strong, and waves of nausea curl inside Kaye's throat as she swallows. She fills another cup with water and guzzles it because Eric has once said that this was the cure for hangover dehydration. She pops three extra-strength painkillers and heads for the shower.

As she steps into the fog of steam and hot water, Kaye considers whether Eleanor's Norse god could have believed her story about being a police detective. She is too tired to think of being embarrassed by her behavior, though she keeps the possibility in the back of her brain. She stays in the shower a long time. Kaye needs to convince Eleanor not to see that drip of a man again. Not because it would decrease her chances of facing the police detective lie, but because Eleanor should stop pretending she could have any sort of future with him. (Had Eleanor already begun to imagine a future with him—isn't that how these things worked?) Her Frank is a good guy, reliable if not romantic. Eleanor's boys are teenagers, and who would want to have to deal with all of that without a man in the house? Finally, Eleanor doesn't seem to grasp the danger of dating the kind of guy who would bring his family along on a date.

Kaye wonders if Eleanor will listen to her. Kaye herself hates listening to Eleanor, especially if she is right.

By the time Kaye gets out of the shower, she decides that she must deal with the cowboy boot issue, as much as she feels that possession is nine-tenths of the law, and that her daughter is being irrational. She wraps herself in an old powder blue terrycloth robe, towels her hair, and crosses the hall to her daughter's room. It is empty and strangely tidy. "Clara!" she calls out. Clara is not downstairs either. She has gone out, probably to report to her little teen girlfriends that her mother is an asshole. Again. To report that her mother is an asshole again.

9

ANNIE THE DOG barks. Eleanor begins to emerge from a dream where she has not finished graduate school, has a young family, and is forced to commute to another city to the university where her advisor now teaches. The dog fur, the wet nose in her face, on her eye, rouses Eleanor from sleep. "No, Annie," she says and the dog retreats from the bed. The light from the windows, brighter than it usually is when she wakes, revives her. She remembers that she has her master's degree diploma buried in a box in the basement somewhere, and does not have small children whose lives would be ruined by her commute to finish her degree. By the clock, it is eleven, and she doesn't remember setting an alarm. It is Saturday, the day after seeing Phil for the first time in so many years, which is the next thing she thinks about, after the dog, after waking up, after her dream. After thinking of Phil, she thinks of Frank, who is nowhere near. She wouldn't want Frank to know she was thinking of Phil.

She hears Frank's footsteps on the stairs. The house is over one hundred years old and creaks as Frank climbs. With her head now under her blanket, Eleanor pretends to be asleep. Annie leaps onto the pillow above Eleanor's head, and traps her under the blanket. Eleanor doesn't move. Frank makes an apologetic noise, as if not wanting to—but really wanting to—disturb her. He sets a mug of coffee on the bedside table. The scent wafts toward Eleanor. Frank stands over her; she can tell, in that strange way one feels a person hovering like a low-wattage electric shadow. Then he leaves and she feels free to bring her head out from under the blanket and to let her thoughts wander back to Phil and the meeting on the previous evening.

There were questions she had wanted to ask him: Are you going to the class reunion? Do you miss being in the military? What do you recall from when we were teenagers?

There are questions she would like to ask now: Why would you meet me at a time when there was every chance that your soon-to-be-ex-wife and your mother-in-law would also be there? Was that meeting really just to hear your daughter sing in a noisy bar for twenty minutes? Was it a test? Were you checking me out to see if I was the same person as the photo? In imaginary conversations there are no real answers.

And then there was Kaye. Next time, Eleanor will give Kaye a drink limit.

Frank interrupts, calling out from downstairs that he is getting ready to leave. Eleanor already knows that Frank is going to play golf with Napoleon. They will spend their time together competing for the best score, and at the same time, talking about how they ought to be playing better. It won't be their best game. It never is their best game. She hears the squeak of Frank's sneakers on the wood floor by the back door, and the clank and crash of his golf clubs as he sets them down. Is he being loud on purpose to get her attention? Or is he just not even trying to be quiet because he thinks she is sleeping? Eleanor believes the noise is all for her benefit, an opportunity for her to not ignore him.

Frank leaves and Eleanor gets out of bed. Downstairs it is quiet in the kitchen, and the strong midday light washes the room from the northern windows. She takes the milk from the refrigerator to put into the coffee Frank had brought her. Frank is the sort of person who doesn't complete a task. In his attempt to do something kind for her, he has forgotten that she takes milk.

What would it be like to invite Phil over to visit? Would Frank be observant? Would he notice the crush she has on Phil? Frank is rarely observant. Eleanor stirs the milk in her coffee absentmindedly with her index finger and drops her hand to her side, where Annie licks it. Annie makes a low, guttural sound, nearly singing out for more, and Eleanor imagines Phil standing there with her, flirtatiously telling her that she shouldn't let the dog lick the coffee from her finger. Then he would make up something ridiculous after that, about licking fingers, and she would laugh. Even this gives her a tingle.

Eleanor's phone vibrates in the pocket of her robe. Kaye's name is on the screen, along with a text about meeting soon for lunch. Kaye wants to hash out the evening with Phil and his family. But Kaye embarrassed Eleanor so much with her police detective act that Eleanor doesn't answer the text. Kaye never understands why she embarrasses her friend.

Just as she is about to check her computer for email, hoping to see something from Phil, Eleanor hears boy feet flapping on the stairs, and a voice that sounds as if it has been ruined by years of cigarette smoking, though it belongs to a seventeen-year-old who has likely never smoked a thing in his life but is allergic to waking up.

"Mom," Eugene says. "Mom, I think I put all of my clothes in the washing machine last night and forgot to put them in the dryer. You weren't here to remind me."

"To remind you?"

"Dad doesn't."

"All in one load?"

"I don't have much."

Eleanor closes her laptop. "Put them in the dryer now." She is feeling frustrated at being interrupted.

"It will take an hour."

"So?"

Eugene looks at her with widening eyes. "I have a study group in thirty minutes. I have no clothes to wear."

"Not even a shirt and pants?"

"It's all in the machine."

Eleanor pictures the balance of her washing machine ruined by every piece of Eugene's clothing, the darks and lights, all mixed together. From upstairs she hears the triumphant shout of her younger son, Liam, "He is NOT wearing my clothes!"

Eugene shakes his head and continues down the stairs to the basement with the slow resolute gait of someone who does not want to do what he is about to do. From her seat at the kitchen island, Eleanor hears Eugene shut the metal dryer door, then watches for him to climb the stairs and appear in the doorway. When he does, his eyes are puffy, his dark, shoulder-length mop of curls frizzed into a halo around his head. She knows it will be a while before she can read her email. She asks him, "Is the dryer on?" Without answering, he turns and makes his way down the steps to the basement again.

>─<─ ─ ─ >─<

ON SUNDAY AFTERNOON, Phil writes to her:

Eleanor, I love the idea of visiting you. Thanks for the invite. It will be a nice break from the crap here at the house. Let me know when your barbecue is. Maybe I should stay the night and we could have some time to really catch up. Talk soon, Phil.

On Monday, Phil's wife begins communications with an email message. Eleanor is sitting with her morning coffee on the bed, with the laptop open. She hears the sparrows outside and puts off breaking up the latest nest. She feels her blood pressure spike as she sees the message from Linda@ . . . She knows who it is.

"Who are you?" Linda writes.

They had barely met. Why would she put out this effort with a divorce imminent? Why care? Does she know the extent of Eleanor's correspondence with Phil?

Usually, this is the time of day, after Frank has left for the commuter train, before the boys go to school, when Eleanor has been writing to Phil. It is a private time, when she can briefly forget that she is married and part of a family. She writes about the people in her neighborhood, the demands her sons make on her, what recipes she has extracted from the newspaper and whether they work out. So far, Phil has been very interested.

The meeting with him to hear his daughter sing had been arranged at the last minute. Does Eleanor want to tell this to Linda? It is not clear, from what Phil has written, how much Linda knows about their correspondence. Eleanor wants to tell the almost-ex that she didn't know she and her mother would be at the concert, and that she was just meeting an old high school friend. The whole meal was not even something Eleanor had thought would happen. *What am I getting into?* She thinks as she prepares to type.

Eleanor knows she spends way too much time wondering what Phil is doing during the day, trying to imagine what his house is like, where his wife's room is in proximity to his, what their conversations are about. Perhaps the awkwardness between the divorcing husband and wife is something they have grown into. Eleanor had only seen it once. He says that she thwarts his attempts to salvage the family dinners by attending the evening church service. He says that he finds her reading self-help books. Does this sound like the portrait of a woman who would send an email? For a moment, Eleanor decides that she will not respond. Then, thirty seconds later, she changes her mind, but she will not do it right away. She is going to think more on it.

She gets out of bed, leaving the sparrows to continue condo building. She hears a faint, low expletive from the other side of Eugene's door as she knocks to tell him he has to get up for school. She watches Liam move toward the bathroom, then back and forth to his own room to get items of clothing and drop them on the floor. Eugene yells from his room, "Five more minutes, Mother." But if Eleanor relents, he will miss the bus and she will get a phone call asking her to drive him to school because it is too far and too late to walk. Every day, as though she is training for an athletic event, she watches the clock, timing her sons' departure to middle and high school. Liam is on time. Eugene is not. Even though he is the older son, Eleanor must regularly push him out the door. Maybe this is because he is the older one, and she has done something different with Liam.

Eleanor waits for them, and in her brain she draws a blank on how to answer Linda's email. Her heart thumps. At last, the boys leave. Now, she wants to be done with the email to Linda.

She wants to write to Linda, "Who do you think you are? How did you get my email address?" But as Eleanor knows, this is too much for now. And if Linda is like Phil—as couples who have been married this long tend to be—she won't answer these questions. Then Eleanor thinks, "I am a big deal." She wants to be a big deal. She will wait just a little longer to answer.

She showers, dresses, and leashes the dog. Annie jumps at the door and then claws at Eleanor's stomach as she tries to bend to put on her shoes. Outside, new pale green shoots are growing in neighbors' flowerbeds because the weather is warming. The sun is strong for May, and she can feel it on her cheeks and arms. Annie pulls forcefully and Eleanor yanks her back to try to correct her behavior. But she is not in the mood to discipline the dog. She knows that Phil's almost-ex has found the emails from a past "other woman." She is not sure how Linda got into Phil's computer. Wouldn't Phil take measures to protect himself?

Eleanor considers the two of them living in the same house because, though the almost-ex wants to leave Phil, she won't move out. Yet he says they have all the divorce papers filed with each other's lawyers. Phil says that she has walked in while he was on the telephone with Eleanor, and she was angry. This, of course, makes the whole thing more exciting for Eleanor, in a dangerous way, she concedes. Linda is a jealous person. Her temper swings, and Phil says this is because she has trouble with her menstrual cycles. Eleanor has never felt this way—the danger and the edginess—in all of her married life with Frank.

Annie sees another dog, something short, white, and fluffy. She crouches into herding mode, with her ears pricked so that just the tips flop forward, and her eyes stare ahead, steady and unblinking. Her tail is parallel to the sidewalk and she pulls at the leash. Eleanor stops. Annie stops. "Does your dog want to play?" the woman holding the leash of the other dog says. The other dog trots blindly toward them as Annie lunges and bares her teeth. Eleanor now has to explain, "She isn't friendly to other dogs." The woman walks a large circle around and away from Annie, glaring at Eleanor as if to say, "You could have warned me." Eleanor drags Annie home.

Inside her kitchen, Eleanor takes a glass of water and sits at her computer. She opens Linda's email. "I am just a friend who grew up with Phil," she replies. "That's all." She nearly writes that she doesn't mean any harm, but stops short of admitting she has done something wrong. Only in her head.

Linda's response is quick, as though she has been there, at her computer, waiting. "I know that. But *who are you?* What do you want? What is going on between you and my husband?"

Had Phil been open about his past affairs? Or simply not been careful? But what is happening now isn't an affair. "Dear Linda," Eleanor writes. "It's not what you think. I have a husband and two sons. And I am aware that you and Phil have a complicated divorce." Wait— scratch the last sentence. "Are still married." Send.

At this point, Eleanor decides not to mention this correspondence to Phil. She wonders what Phil has said to his almost-ex, and about which one of them—husband or wife— is more truthful. Then she goes off to sort clothes for the laundry. The piles are smaller than usual, Eugene having recently done his own. She puts on talk radio but doesn't pay attention to it. Then, at the computer, she writes to Linda, "What is it you want from me?" as if this distraction is overwhelming her attention.

Whether from at work or home, Linda is still answering. "You ought to know," she writes to Eleanor, "that he has left a trail of women."

"I am not interested in Phil that way," Eleanor writes back.

"They have all said that. But I've seen it before. He sucks it all in, and forgets, and someday it will explode. I'll be there to pick up the pieces for him, married to him or not. There is a list of women Phil has left behind. He tosses them in my face, like he did at the club, while our daughter was singing.

"I don't understand why you were there to hear her play," Linda continues to write. "Even if Phil asked you to come, why would you do that when I was there and my mother was there?"

Eleanor is now feeling guilty and manipulated. She doesn't quite understand Linda's intent, though she does understand Phil's. She thinks she understands the idea of a safe relationship, a friendship under the watch of their families. She writes back that Phil only invited her because she lives in town, that she brought her friend, that she didn't know the rest of the family would be there. Then she stops. How do you convince someone who is likely inconvincible? She deletes what she has written. Linda emails, "I'm praying for you." And suddenly, just as quickly as she had appeared online, she is gone.

10

ELEANOR IS SLEEPY from the two glasses of wine she drank at lunch. She wouldn't call herself drunk. Tipsy maybe. At home on the computer she writes, "Phil, what happened the other night? Why so many members of your soon-to-be estranged family? My girlfriend thinks that you and I are going to sleep together. In fact, she is convinced of it. I told her that this would be impossible because I am married to Frank and absorbed in the lives of my kids." She stops typing and thinks about her lunch with Kaye at the plaza near the lake. They'd sat at the tables on the sidewalk patio, where they could see the lake between the high-rise condos across Sheridan Road. High-rise, by Wilmette standards.

"It isn't completely out of the range of possibility," she continues to write. "I am forty-eight. But I exercise to keep fit and I color my hair to hide the grey. I am not unattractive. Sometimes I want to ask my husband, 'Honey, do you think I am still attractive?' But he would look at me and say, 'You might as well ask me if you look fat. What am I supposed to say?' Isn't there more than just how you look? Pheromones perhaps? Or animal magnetism? Do you sense this about me? Am I magnetic?"

At lunch, Eleanor and Kaye had both ordered sandwiches, gazpacho, and white wine, and before the drinks even arrived, Kaye had said, "What the heck was that all about?" referring to the meeting with Phil. "Who brings a family to see his old girlfriend?"

Eleanor had replied that she was not Phil's old girlfriend. "We were just friends."

Now she deletes the email and begins again. "Phil, do you really have lawyers putting your divorce together?" Kaye had rolled her eyes when Eleanor explained, once again, that Phil's wife was living in the same house while she looked for her own. "Why is your wife living with you if she has left you? And don't tell me it's to save money. Is your divorce really happening?" Eleanor types. "You know, she emailed me the other day, sort of a territory-marking activity, I would say." And then she adds, "Like my dog would do."

Just as the sun became hot over their bacon, lettuce, and tomato, Eleanor had explained to Kaye, "I didn't realize we'd go to a club, watch his kid sing, and then go out to eat afterward with his wife and mother-in-law." She wonders how she may have misread Phil's signals, that after the twenty minutes of hearing Jillian play, should she have taken Kaye and gone home? "Did we do something wrong?" she asked Kaye.

Kaye had answered her, "Remember my idea to go as your lesbian girlfriend to your high school reunion?"

"I do," Eleanor replied. "I really shouldn't listen to you."

"Your wife," she writes to Phil, "wants me to leave you alone. She says you have had many women and that you leave a trail of them behind you. This doesn't seem like the Phil I remember, whose parents remained married while their children were in high school, who dated the same girl for two long years, even went to college with her before breaking up. Now I wonder myself why I am getting involved with someone like this. Please convince me that there are no other women 'friends.' Why would your wife lie to me? I can think of many reasons why she would, but with nothing going on between us now, why does she even care? She says that she is praying for me." Delete.

"Phil, there is nothing I hate more than a woman who says she is praying for me. I don't think of myself as the kind of person who needs to be prayed over. I thought I was a helpful sort of person. I used to volunteer at my kids' school for hours a week, but I got burned out. I am burned out from being a wife." Delete. Delete.

Kaye's voice is in the back of Eleanor's head. Their lunch conversation had become heated. "You do so want to sleep with him. And why not? He's a Norse god."

Eleanor had answered, somewhat too seriously, "That's not enough, Kaye."

She types. "No one I know seems to pay attention to me the way that you do. If you would just say that what you really want is to sleep with me, then I would feel good psychologically and then we wouldn't actually have to do it." Again, delete.

Eleanor tries to think about the last time Frank wanted her spontaneously rather than out of necessity. She tries to think of the last time she wanted Frank, or when she wanted someone other than Phil. She comes up blank.

"Dear Phil, how is your garden? Have any good vegetables ripened yet? I have never had a garden here. The house is a hundred years old, and I have learned that there is lead paint in the soil around it, and that it takes centuries to biodegrade.

So, we only have flowers, and the dog tramples them over. The yard looks terrible. There are kicked up piles of dirt along a path where she runs. Still, I am having a cookout dinner party in the yard next weekend. Will you come?" Press: send.

IT'S THE MIDDLE of the night and Phil can't sleep. This is a chronic problem now. No sex, no sleep, no comfort, no warmth, no love. He gets up and walks around the bedroom in the darkness, watching the shadows that the outside light casts on the rumpled bedclothes. Finally, he crosses the hallway to the stairs and down to the kitchen. Phoenix is lying on the slatted wood floor on her side, legs out. He startles her as he turns on the light. She raises her head and he bends down to pat it. "Hey, girl." He fills a glass of water and drinks like he has been thirsty for hours and the water will make him sleep. Then he fills Phoenix's water bowl. In the kitchen window, he sees his reflection in the night blackness of the glass, blurry and wavering as he shifts from one leg to the other.

From the hallway of the house, he can hear the white noise of the refrigerator. His daughter's door is closed. His wife is in the guest room off the living room, he presumes. Her door is also closed. Simeon the cat is asleep on his back near the family room couch. Phil can see Simeon from where he is standing, his white cat chest gently rising and falling, legs quivering at an awkward position half in the air. Phil has never seen another cat sleep in this way. For a dog, it would be a signal that he is comfortable enough to show his belly. But Phil doesn't know what this means for a cat.

He thinks of the visit to Eleanor and her barbecue. How will she see him when he arrives alone, not surrounded by his family as he was at their last meeting? Will she think of him as someone incapable of keeping a family together? He has a knot in his stomach. He drinks more water and opens his computer, which is sitting on the kitchen island, recharging.

Phil begins to write. The internet is a thread connecting him to someone who will listen and sympathize, and it feels like a direct conversation, in the moment, even though it is not. He is aware that some days it doesn't matter if it is Eleanor or someone else.

Hi Eleanor, I know I mentioned that my wife is leaving me, that we are trying to split amicably so that we can remain friends and still share the business together, that at night we sit at the table in the dining room with all of our assets spread out on sheets of paper, and a calendar open. Sometimes she won't say anything to me but to answer my questions with a single word or sound. Sometimes she cries and I can't reach her from where I am sitting to comfort her, and I think she is the one who has put that distance between us so that she can't change her mind about leaving me. But I didn't exactly tell you the whole story.

No. Wrong. Delete.

Eleanor, my wife and I are getting divorced. I have told you some of this before. She has a friend she is with constantly, and I can't watch them together anymore. He comes to our house. He drives her to church. They don't touch each other in public, but I don't know what they are doing when I am not around. And I have seen his text messages. About how he wants to hold her hand or sit with her or put his arm around her when she cries. I wouldn't have written that sort of crap to a girl when I was in high school. I have tried to convince her to come back. I want to say to her, 'You don't have to do this.' But now the words feel stuck inside me. I don't really say anything to her.

Too much information? Does she need to know this much? Delete.

Dear Eleanor, I don't want to give you the wrong impression of me, that I am the same person I was when we were in high school, that I didn't grow up and change. My wife wouldn't sleep with me anymore, so I found Sarayu and Linda saw the emails. That is why Linda gets upset when you and I talk or email. Yet it doesn't occur to her that her friend—the guy she goes with to church—isn't going to bother me? That her shift from a non-believing Catholic to attending a Protestant megachurch with a man who is ten years younger doesn't seem a bit strange? You bet it's strange. I can't emphasize enough how strange it is to me.

Delete again. He sits back, puts his hands behind his head, elbows out, stretches, breathes, sips more water. He clears his mind. The page is blank. The refrigerator kicks on again. Phoenix rolls onto her other side, flipping her legs into the air, then sighs deeply, sounding human. Once again Phil feels as though he doesn't have the right words to say what he wants to say. Something like, will you still be there, at the other end of this computer connection, in your home with your family, when you find out who I really am?

Eleanor, I am hoping we can have time to talk and catch up when I see you again. I have a lot to tell you. Can't wait to see you on the weekend.

He presses send and logs out. Phoenix raises her head and watches him as he pads out of the kitchen, then returns to her former position. Upstairs, Phil lies in his bed and stares at the ceiling for what seems like an hour, until there is light through the thin, vertical spaces between the curtain panels, until he feels his eyes close and eventually he doesn't know that he is falling asleep.

TRAFFIC HAS BEEN thick and slow. Stopped in his car, Phil texts Eleanor, "I'm running late. Sorry."

"No worries," she answers.

He gets to the final stoplight and looks for a parking spot. He can see the source of the traffic jam: people moving their cars in and out of parking spaces along the two-lane street. He taps on the steering wheel impatiently.

He is late because of Linda. He honestly hadn't expected her to react so strongly. "You are the one who wants the divorce," he had said, as she found reason after reason for him to stay home. He wanted to say, "For Christ's sake! I'm visiting her family." But he avoided Eleanor's name or anything about her for that matter.

While Phil looked at his wife, who stood with her mouth wide, her hands splayed, pleading, everything about her body exuding anger and hurt, he suddenly wondered about Sarayu and how she must have looked and felt when she read the email he had written to her to say that it was all over. It wasn't something he had let himself think about in a long time. In Linda's place, he saw Sarayu's dark brown eyes, glossy with tears, the shape of her shoulders curved inward, her upper body slumped as she put her head in her hands. Then he saw Eleanor and thought of how he would have to explain himself to her, and that he was sorry for his mistakes. Would she listen? Would she offer him forgiveness?

But, Linda . . . she'd left him speechless. Should he say that she was right, "Yes, it's my fault. Please say you won't leave me. Water under the bridge?" But how much could he change, realistically?

As he opened his mouth to say something, and these thoughts flooded his head, the words were stuck. And once he realized that he had nothing to say to his wife, nothing that she wanted to hear, he picked up his overnight bag and walked out the door to his car. He left. Now he is here, just west of Evanston, waiting for the traffic to abate. What is he doing?

11

ON THE MORNING after Phil's email, Sarayu quit her job as a traveling RN. In a phone call, she told her boss that she had a family emergency in Toronto. She packed a small suitcase and took her car to the mechanic for an oil change and tire rotation. When she picked up her car, she leaned her head on the steering wheel and tears poured from her eyes. The mechanic knocked on the window and asked if she was all right, and could she move her car?

She drove north toward Wisconsin, away from the north-western Illinois towns where she had traveled for work. She did not go to Toronto and her family. What would she say to them? That she had been in a relationship with a married man? Her grandmother had grown up in India. What would she say to her? And Sarayu's sister, married and raising her two young boys?

Now, driving into Wisconsin, she faced her obsession with Phil, her embarrassment over the sex in motel rooms, in dark, secret places.

Sarayu wanted to forget their first meeting, going to Phil's home. His family was away. He had grilled salmon and they drank a lot of wine. She felt a trancelike state of sexuality.

When they walked in the darkness along the river, she went into a nearby thicket and took off her clothes. As she slipped into the water, she knew he was watching her. Her boldness surprised him.

At a truck stop near Green Bay, she bought two bottles of cheap wine.

That evening, drunk from the wine, she tried her best not to telephone Phil. But when she did, his daughter answered, and Sarayu hung up, suddenly frightened of what she had done, and by her inability to control herself. She didn't know how much Phil's wife and family knew about the affair. She had never called his home before.

Waking up in a sweat and tearful, she could hear the air conditioner hum and the pounding of children's feet on the carpeted hallway. She dozed. At one point she thought Phil was there in the motel room with her. She took some Ativan.

In the morning, Sarayu woke with a hangover. She made coffee, placing the premeasured filter pack in the coffee maker and filling the machine with water. There was something calming about following the simple instructions, when she was far away from her problems. She drank the coffee and peered out the window between the drapes at the untended field beyond the parking lot. She felt the compulsion to check her phone, even though she had blocked Phil's number.

She threw her bag in the back of the car and filled the gas tank at a nearby station. She continued her journey north, without checking the rearview mirror.

The following morning, in northern Minnesota, Sarayu woke without a hangover. She showered, and, in her mind, she tested herself. She thought about Phil. Her pulse did not increase. Her head felt clear. She stood naked in front of the bathroom mirror. Her summer tan lines had faded and her skin was an even tone. As she smoothed her wet hair with a brush, she could feel the tension of the plastic bristles against her scalp. She dressed in a T-shirt and jeans and went to the lobby for breakfast.

Over coffee and a hard-boiled egg, she watched young children insert bread in the toaster and pour milk over cereal. She saw adults absorbed in newspapers or the broadcast on the television set attached to a wall. A hotel server refilled her coffee, and as she said thank you, she did not recognize the voice that came from deep in her throat.

Sarayu was thirty-seven years old. She had never wanted to have children. She had been independent for a long time. Even while seeing Phil, she had kept to her own schedule, which was often complicated.

Back in her room, she checked the emails and messages from her friends at home on her phone. Of course, there was nothing from Phil. She took a deep breath and decided that this was good, that her friends cared about her. She took time to send answers, that she was coming home, an estimate of when she would be there. She used the hair dryer to fix her hair. She put on a face moisturizer and hand cream, lipstick and a sweater, and straightened herself out before folding dirty clothes into her suitcase. Then she did a once-over to see that she had packed everything.

At the desk she asked for directions to the nearest gas station, where she filled the tank, washed the windows, and checked the windshield wiper fluid. She still carried the physical ache of rejection. She knew it wasn't just Phil, but perhaps a series of similar instances with men who could not commit, who would not interfere with her independence, who would not want children or the life her grandmother and sister had chosen. Out on the highway, she drove toward Chicago and her apartment. It was time to be independent again. It was time to go.

DRIVING SOUTH FROM Green Bay, Sarayu noticed the trees were yellow and orange and dotted with brown leaves. Fall. She had not noticed them on the drive north, as if they had changed completely in a few days. Now she saw rows and rows of dried cornstalks crumpled in the fields.

At the point where she reached the edge of the Milwaukee suburbs, she could not help but think of the time she had met Phil at the Milwaukee Art Museum, a white, skeletal structure that imitated the riggings of a boat. On that spring day it had been unusually cold, and she wore a winter coat over a silk blouse and a skirt, thinking he might take her to dinner after the museum. But in the end, the museum was merely a meeting place before going to a hotel. She saw him waiting at the entrance and flew at him. He caught her in an embrace that made her think they were really in love. "I'm right here," he had said. They wandered briefly through a Frank Lloyd Wright exhibit, pretending to concentrate on the drawings and floor plans of various homes and businesses, holding hands while they looked at paintings of uncomfortable chairs in tall, empty watercolor-washed spaces. It was so much like the college romances she'd had, where she and the boy whose hand she held only thought about each other as they wandered the concrete campus, through crowds of students. At least, this was what she remembered. Afterward, when Phil took her to the hotel, he didn't want to go out to dinner, and she stupidly agreed. They ate cold room service on top of the sheets. It had been another one of those times with him where she felt hidden away, even in a city far from his own. At the time she could not articulate how much the whole thing bothered her. Instead, she let him decide how things would be. This way, it had helped her not to think about his wife and daughter, or about her own family, about the layers of disapproval.

She drove along the beltway of Milwaukee, past industrial buildings colored by soot and age, and snaked along a skyway in between them, billboards lining the roadway as if sticking up from nowhere. Eventually the roads forked, one way west toward where Phil lived, the other back home to Chicago.

NOW THAT SHE had quit her job, she had time to clean her apartment and throw out the rancid food. She kept busy, meeting friends for coffee, lunch, dinner. She filled her calendar, and friends assumed she was simply taking a vacation between jobs. Or they did not altogether understand why she had quit something she had seemed to enjoy. She had never told them that the part of traveling for her job that she loved most had been spending time with Phil. Instead she simply said that she didn't want to stay in another hotel. She wanted to be home. This her friends accepted without question. In fact, upon arriving home, she never wanted to smell the starch of hotel sheets or the dry floral scent of hotel soap. She never again wanted to eat takeout or room service on top of a bed. She didn't want to ever worry if the man she was seeing felt the same way about her as she did about him, or about the consequences of what she was doing to his family.

Gradually, she willed herself not to remember his face, or his eyes, or the difference in color and size of their clasped hands. She did not look at couples walking entwined together on the streets of her Andersonville neighborhood, or sitting on the same side of a booth in a restaurant. She no longer had anything to remind her of Phil in her apartment, on her computer, or her phone. She tried, in the middle of the night, to read *The Economist* when she woke up thinking about him, and to forget him so that he was not a part of her anymore in the times when she could not control her thoughts. Soon, she would find that she had gone a whole lunch with a girlfriend, or a dinner in front of a television program, without him popping into her thoughts.

And things began to settle down.

12

THE TREES ARE old and full along Central Street. They make tiny movements that shift and filter light from the west, casting transient shadows on the pavement. Kaye watches out the window of a coffee and gelato shop on the south side of the street. She has come to pass the time with a newspaper in the hope that her daughter might walk past. Surprisingly, instead of Clara and her teen girlfriends, Kaye spots the Norse god. At first, she is uncertain. She has only met him once. But when he stands next to his Alfa Romeo, trying to use the credit-card parking meter, she gets a better look. She is not one to forget faces. He is wearing tight jeans and tries to put his wallet into his back pocket with some difficulty. This makes Kaye laugh. When he turns in her direction, she bows her head and hides behind the open newspaper, looking up to see him cross the street. She leaves her latte on the counter and exits the café to follow him.

Phil goes to the florist. Kaye lingers on the sidewalk outside, looking at displays of large, glazed planter pots and ornate wrought iron garden chairs, all covered with plants. She moves, trying not to be obvious, to the store next door. But the filmy sundresses and platform shoes in the window make her feel old.

Eventually she enters the florist. It is dark and filled with the wet earthy smell of just-watered plants. Phil is talking to the shop girl and gesturing with his credit card in his hand. They share a joke. He begins to face Kaye, but she simultaneously turns her back to him and picks up a potted succulent. Phil looks directly at her but says nothing. Either he doesn't see her face, or he doesn't recognize her. Kaye hears the wrinkle of tissue paper, the credit card processing, and small talk she would never remember if asked. Then, Phil is on his way out, and she catches his cologne, not unpleasant but strong. She whispers, "I told you so, Eleanor," to herself. Glancing at the young woman behind the counter, a contemporary of Clara's, her first thought is to wonder if Phil had been flirting with her. She is sickened by the idea.

ELEANOR STANDS AT the sink, deveining shrimp. A fishy smell hovers over the kitchen. She feels like kicking herself for choosing a shrimp appetizer. But the shrimp, and then the chicken marinating in the fridge, will keep Frank busy at his grill. She stops a moment to check her hands. Fish. What man wants a fishy woman?

But no. No. Nothing will happen with Phil. So, what does it matter? Even so, nervous, sweaty, she scrubs the sink and then takes the brush and scrubs her hands. Annie paws her leg. She knows about the fish. To her, fish smell is good.

With the shrimp skewered, seasoned, and sitting in a baking pan in the refrigerator, she opens the window and increases the speed of the ceiling fan, then goes upstairs to shower and change into a sundress. Already this makes her feel calmer. Back in the kitchen, the fish smell is dissipating. She can tell because the dog has gone.

It is late afternoon, and the boys will be home soon from school. In their usual Friday routine, they will go straight to their computers without saying hello or giving Eleanor a chance to ask about their day. They will begin to play war games. Sometimes they even play these games against each other, sitting in the same room and only communicating through their computers. But she does not necessarily know that this is happening when she walks past and looks and sees their eyes on the laptop screens.

Eleanor puts a bottle of red wine on the counter and two whites in the fridge. She has made a jug of her own peppermint iced tea to have early, so that she doesn't get drunk with Phil before Frank even gets home. Everything is prepped, and now she awaits Phil's arrival. In her pocket, she feels her phone buzz. It is a text from Phil. He will be late.

PHIL DRIVES ALONG a grid of tree-lined streets under a canopy of branches and leaves that block the sun, past large, century-old homes and groomed lawns. It is different from the sparse treescape and new homes that abut the cornfields where he lives. Eleanor is waiting on her porch steps wearing a blue sundress and sandals, holding her phone like she has been there some time. Her hair is against her shoulders, moving in the light wind. She rests her chin on the palm of her hand, her elbow propped on her knee, as she watches his car pull up under a tree in front of her house. For a moment, he thinks that he remembers her in this pose in high school. He remembers someone like this.

"Hey!" he calls to her as he gets out of his car and reaches into the passenger side for the bouquet. He knows it seems ridiculous, but he feels tongue-tied. Eleanor is grinning as if she has just heard a sarcastic joke. He walks to her, throws his arms around her and squeezes tight. She gasps as she is released.

"How was the drive?"

"Fine." He puts the flowers into her hands and her face turns to a deep pink. He sees that she is embarrassed. But she seems to catch herself and asks, "Can I help you bring in your bags?" He tells her no.

At the door, a small black-and-white border collie greets him with a sniff and a low growl, baring her teeth before running away. Eleanor apologizes for the dog and takes him to the kitchen where they sit on stools at the island. She pours two glasses of iced tea. The house feels empty and quiet to Phil, and the iced tea is bitter. He wants to find an amusing, provocative way to ask her for sugar, some play with words, but all that comes out is, "Do you have sweetener?"

Eleanor looks puzzled for a moment, and nods and climbs onto a stool to reach inside an upper cabinet for a paper sack of cooking sugar, then walks near the sink for a spoon. "Take this."

He smiles and mixes a spoonful of sugar into his tea.

Eleanor is full of questions and Phil doesn't know how to answer them and still appear as though he is not too serious. "Did your family seem upset that you were coming here alone? What did Linda say? You didn't have to argue with her, did you?"

He assumes she is asking because of the awkwardness he

has told her about and his text about being late. But still, it seems strange, almost as if Linda has spoken to her. He shakes his head and looks into his glass. "No, really, in the end it was fine." He smiles shyly, wanting to keep the conversation upbeat, positive.

Eleanor takes Phil back to the front of the house where he discovers that her sons are at home, logged on to their computers. "I never would have known," he says.

"They sneak in and get online to play war games before I can say anything," she says.

Eugene and Liam look up as if wakened from a deep sleep. Phil puts out his hand to shake, and, one after the other, they take it with what seems like skepticism. Phil has seen this sort of behavior before, the stunned acceptance of an adult gesture. He laughs nervously, though he senses that Eleanor is more uncomfortable with their reluctance than he is.

"Come on," Eleanor says, and turns away. She picks up Phil's bag near the front door and takes it upstairs. "I'll show you your room."

They climb the stairs. In the small corridor of the second floor, Eleanor points to the closed doors. "That's Liam's room. The one there is Eugene's. Then the bathroom you'll use. I left towels on your bed." She hesitates. "This is my room. I mean, my room with Frank. And next door, this," she puts the bag inside the door, "is yours."

As Phil enters the room, the dog exits the master bedroom, stops, shows her teeth to Phil, and trots down the stairs. Phil pretends not to notice the dog. He stands for a moment next to one of the twin beds and puts his bag on top of the other while Eleanor steps into the doorframe. "Great!" he says, not referring to the dog, and waiting for Eleanor's cue. When it doesn't come, and he needs to fill the airspace, he says, "Could I have another glass of iced tea?"

"Sure."

She turns quickly and heads down the stairs. Phil is put off by her aloofness, and yet it intrigues him. He follows her down the warm corridor.

"Frank should be home any minute," she mutters so that Phil can barely hear her.

"I could help with dinner, if you want," he calls after her, wondering if he has done something wrong and misinterpreted this visit, or if she is playing hard to get.

LATER, PHIL, ELEANOR, and Frank are in the kitchen. Phil smiles artificially—he knows it—trying to keep the mood upbeat as he gently tears lettuce leaves from a colander to put into the salad bowl. Eleanor is at the sink washing dishes, and Frank is trying to put marinated chicken pieces from a plastic container onto a platter to take outside. "You don't think you over-marinated the meat, El?" There is a puddle of teriyaki sauce on the counter around the plate. He steps back and turns to Phil, smiling as if he is setting up camaraderie between the two men.

Trying to think up good conversation, Phil asks, "How far are you from the beach?"

"Two miles," Frank says. Eleanor doesn't turn around.

"Do you go much?"

Eleanor shrugs her shoulders. "She used to take the boys when they were young," Frank says. "But they went in opposite directions and she spent all of her time running after them." He has his teriyaki hands in one of the utensil drawers shuffling things around.

"Frank, wash your hands," Eleanor says.

He laughs and continues to talk. "It used to be sort of fun in those days. Chasing them around."

"When I was stationed in Southern California," Phil says, "we were at the beach all the time. I loved open water swimming."

Eleanor turns to look Phil in the eye, as though she is impressed, or thinks that he is crazy. Phil can't tell. "Well," she says, "this isn't the ocean."

Phil's phone vibrates in his pocket. He takes it out and, after a second, he recognizes Sarayu's number. His phone is always on vibrate in case his daughters should call him, but the strangeness of this particular call shocks him. He completely loses his place in the conversation and doesn't know what to do. Suddenly, for a moment, he feels as though he is emptied out. Should he leave and find a private place to take the call? He decides to wait and call back but knows that he will be able to think of little else.

"Anyone good?" Frank asks.

"Naw," Phil answers. He looks to Eleanor, who turns from the sink toward the men. He doesn't catch her eye, or she won't look at him. Maybe she thinks Linda is checking up.

"Come with me," she says to Phil. He follows her to the basement to carry folding chairs up to the patio in the backyard. Like someone uncoordinated, he stumbles as he thinks over what is happening. "Watch out," Eleanor says, and it embarrasses him. He is here to see one woman, and another from his past is calling him. Sarayu must hate him now, that must be why she is calling. There is a buzz on his phone to indicate that she has left a message. He can't imagine what it might be, but now he needs to know.

To try to think about something else, he asks Eleanor who else is coming, and remarks about the calmness of the weather, the warmth, how dinner outside is such a good idea, and again he asks who is coming. He helps Eleanor to set up a large folding table where the guests will sit. They cover it with a floral tablecloth and put citronella candles on top. There is a warm wind in the backyard. He draws his hand across his forehead involuntarily. Eleanor smiles at him. "Are you all right?"

"Yes." But he feels pangs of anxiety. How could Sarayu call right now? Right now? He needs to know what she has to say to him. Maybe she isn't as angry as he thinks she should be. He can't make a judgment until he hears her message, though he is making all sorts of things up in his head, that she forgives him, that she wants to see him, that she wants him dead. He looks over the mangled vegetation around the edge of the yard and garden. Annie, Eleanor's dog, tramples it, back and forth, barking at something on the other side of the fence, and inside his head he hears himself explaining things to Sarayu. It was the only thing to do, to break up. He has a wife. Daughters. What other choice was there? He looks up, feels flushed. Frank is coming out the back door and Eleanor is going inside to boil potatoes. She says so as she walks toward the stairs to the door, with one provocative look back at Phil. He follows her just as Frank asks him if he wants a beer from the cooler on the patio. "I need to check my calls first," Phil says, and goes inside. He can wait no longer. And Eleanor can wait.

In his room upstairs, he listens to Sarayu's message. "I thought I would check to see how you are," is all that she says. Strangely, he is only a few miles away from her Andersonville apartment. She could have sent a text, but he recalls that she hates texting. Once again, the feeling of heat overcomes him. He sits on the bed. These coincidences are something out of a movie or a cheap novel. He tries to compose himself for the dinner party. He needs to be on his best behavior. He needs to impress Eleanor. He remembers this feeling, the physical sensation of alertness, he felt it when he was about to see Eleanor for the first time in years. But with Sarayu, it is different. He knows that he has hurt her deeply.

"Phil?"

Eleanor is calling from the bottom of the stairs.

"Right there in a moment." He breathes in deeply and heads toward the kitchen. "Calls from my girls." He smiles awkwardly. Lying is still easiest.

13

"YOU READY TO help me fire up the grill?" Frank asks. He hands Phil one of two cookie sheets that contain marinated chicken pieces. They move toward the back door, which Frank pushes unsteadily open, and down the steps to the patio. Outside the air is moist, and Phil can smell the grass clippings from the newly mowed lawn next door. He follows Frank and puts his tray on a metal table near the cooker. Frank opens the lid and takes out a steel brush to clean the grill.

"We'll just heat this barbecue up."

Frank reaches into a cooler and hands Phil a beer. "Twist-off," he says as he opens his own.

"Thanks."

"So, you are in town to visit your daughter at Northwestern tomorrow?"

"Yes. It was nice of you and your wife to let me stay over."

"What is she majoring in?"

Phil laughs. "History. Not sure what she will do with it."

Frank nods. "Like English. Eleanor did nothing with it. She had babies."

"That worked out, didn't it?"

"Tell me something," Frank says. "Do you really remember details from high school?"

Phil feels the blood hot in his face. He drinks and laughs nervously. "Sure."

"I remember almost nothing. Eleanor says she remembers what I was wearing when we met."

"I remember Eleanor. She was a nice person."

Frank's smile flattens. He sips his beer. "That's not a detail. That's a generalization." Then he pauses and slaps Phil on the shoulder. Phil loses his balance before straightening. For a moment he wonders what he is doing here, other than on the way to see Jilly. He remembers the anger in his almost-ex-wife's voice as he left their house. "I was going out with someone else then, for a couple of years," Phil tells him, feeling self-conscious.

Frank nods and runs the flat of his hand inches above the slats of the grill. "That's what Eleanor said." He smiles. "She would never have gone out with someone like you. Not then. She was too shy."

"Yes."

"So, what is it you do?"

"I have a leasing and service company for copiers and computers. But things are slow right now. I have time to visit my kid."

Eleanor is still preparing food in the kitchen. Phil hears voices from the other side of the screen door, lilting first greetings, and he sees the shadow before a tall blonde woman appears in the doorway. She stops to take in the scene. Phil remembers her from his daughter's concert, the police detective. She walks straight toward him with her right hand outstretched, and Phil takes it. A shorter man with a large belly follows her, carrying a plate of raw vegetables and dips. "Hello again," she says to Phil. "Kaye? I met you at the concert?"

"And I'm the one with the funny accent. I'm Eric. I go with her."

"How's the force?" Phil asks Kaye.

"That," she says, almost whispering. "Fine. Not much excitement right now. Summer isn't quite here."

"My ex-wife seemed to enjoy talking to you."

Kaye looks at him. Her mouth is open. "I thought you weren't divorced yet."

"Only a matter of semantics."

Kaye rolls her eyes and reaches into the cooler. "You want another?" Phil holds out his hand and she gives him a beer. "So, you aren't driving home tonight?"

"No. I am staying over and seeing my daughter in the morning. The one who played the concert."

"What did you do this afternoon?" she asks him. "Did Eleanor take you to the lake? It was a nice day for that sort of thing."

Phil looks toward Frank as he steps away from the grill. He and Eric are drinking beer and talking about something that is making them laugh. Phil feels ill at ease, and he is still distracted by Sarayu's phone call, wondering what she meant by it. Then he looks at Kaye. "The waterfront? No. Only seen it from the car closer to the university. When I come here, I see my daughter and I don't stay long."

"Really. Do you sail? The university has boat rentals."

"I did in California. When I was first married."

"My husband, Eric, is building a boat. The guy over there. The joker." She points with her beer bottle. "He wants to call his boat the *God of Thunder*."

"Don't boats usually have female names?"

"There you go," Kaye says sarcastically. "It's a Viking boat. The kind Erik the Red sailed from Scandinavia. Supposedly. Eric the Grey here will sail a Viking boat around Lake Michigan. And when it is in the water and I am sitting there with him, people will stare at us as we try to sail the damned thing out of the harbor."

"Is he Scandinavian? I'm Scandinavian."

"Are you now? I never would have guessed. You don't have an accent. No, he's from Scotland."

"I mean my great grandparents came from Scandinavia."

"Kaye," Eric says to his wife, "Go and find out where the hostess is. We're hungry!"

Phil listens to Frank talking to Eric about a recent golf game. He smiles when he thinks it's appropriate, and when Frank asks, he says that he is not much of a golfer. "Why not?" Frank says. "You look so goddamned athletic."

"Did you come with someone, Phil?" Eric asks, as though he has missed something.

"Phil's divorced!" Frank says. "He is an old high school friend of my wife's, right Phil?"

"Another beer?" Eric asks, holding out a newly opened bottle to Phil.

"Sure."

"And his daughter is a student at Northwestern," Frank offers. "He's just visiting for the night."

Eric winks and drinks from his beer.

"I'm seeing her tomorrow," Phil says. "I met your wife when she came to my daughter's concert a couple of weeks ago."

"You did?" Eric raises his eyebrows. "She sure gets around, that woman does." Frank and Eric laugh and Phil tries to as well. Then Eric laughs harder. He must have a private joke with Frank to which Phil doesn't have access.

"Your wife told me about being a police detective," Phil says. "In the vice squad."

Eric stops drinking. He is silent. Then he bursts into hilarious laughter. "Are we talking about the same woman?"

"Is that what she told you?" Frank is also enjoying the joke.

"OH! LORD!" Eric says. He slaps his knee, then Frank's back, as though he needs to hit things. "Not again!"

Phil is embarrassed. As if to be sympathetic, Frank reaches into the cabinet below the grill and pulls out a bottle and small bathroom-sized Dixie cups with the Muppets pictured on the sides. "Here." He pours and laughs and shakes his head, handing Phil a cup of whisky. "I think you need this after hanging out with Kaye."

KAYE ENTERS THE kitchen through the back door. "Where the hell have you been? We are out there making conversation with your fifth wheel."

Eleanor is putting things on a tray to bring outside. She doesn't stop puttering to answer.

"You're nervous, aren't you," Kaye says.

Eleanor looks up at her friend. "No."

"I saw him today at the florist. He is a huge flirt. He was hitting on the girl working there. She is Clara's age." Kaye is exaggerating, she knows, but she wants to give Eleanor a warning of some kind. She doesn't like or trust Phil.

"How do you know how old the girl at the florist is?"

"I can tell."

"Let him have his fun. It doesn't hurt anyone."

"Doesn't he flirt with you? Isn't that what this whole thing is?"

"No." Eleanor's voice is firm.

Kaye is taken aback. She recalls the time, maybe seven years ago, when she tried to tell a friend that she thought her husband was drunk when he drove to pick up his daughter from a playdate. Her friend told her to mind her own business. And somehow, Kaye felt that she had done the right thing. Here, she feels it's right to warn Eleanor, in case she and Phil were having ideas about each other. He had, after all, driven an hour and a half to visit.

Eleanor looks at Kaye. "Oh Christ, Kaye. It's only dinner."

ELEANOR AND KAYE come out carrying trays of chips and condiments, wine and glasses. They set these things on the table, and Eleanor goes inside for more.

"Can I help?" Phil takes the opportunity to leave Eric and Frank, desperate to find a place where he cannot hear them giggling like schoolgirls, and where he doesn't have to answer questions or be the butt of their jokes.

In the kitchen, Eleanor nods. "Did you figure out that Kaye's not a cop? I hope you aren't offended. She likes to play games."

"Not a problem," Phil says.

Suddenly, Eleanor seems to have nothing to say. She looks at him, then down at the food laid out on the island, and back up again. He is a distraction. His knit shirt fits snugly on his chest without the doughy rolls of her husband and Eric, who have both sunk into the graceless form of middle age, of train commuters who don't work out. He smiles genuinely at her. He seems happy to be here. He is a good guest, offering to help. And it's hard not to stare at him, to think that she never would have imagined him coming over to her house when she was in high school.

"What?" Phil asks, with nothing else to say.

"Nothing." She smiles. "Help me to bring this outside. I'm sure you're hungry after standing next to the grill."

Phil turns toward the screened windows to the patio where the others are laughing again. He gestures for her to go ahead of him and giggles uncomfortably. He wants her to like him, this woman who is comfortably situated in her suburb, with a decent husband, children, friends. She isn't getting a divorce because she cheated. And yet, she listens to him. In fact, she seems like the kind of woman who would not cheat, but then that is how Sarayu was, and then his wife. Phil wants Eleanor to like him, to approve of him. Beyond that, he isn't sure. She represents to him the past, when marriage didn't seem so complicated.

Frank calls from outside. "Eleanor! Chicken is about ready! Start pouring the wine!" Eleanor pauses a moment, to think that maybe he could have reached over to the table to pour it himself, but he is too busy with Eric. She doesn't enjoy being told what to do.

Phil waits because he has nothing to say, even though he wishes that he did. He is sure that Frank can't see them from outside. Together, Phil and Eleanor bring out the trays with salads and plates. Eugene and Liam come outside, then they all sit at a long table piled with food.

ERIC WATCHES PHIL pass the salad bowl to Kaye, enjoying himself, knowing that Kaye is annoyed with Phil. She presses her lips together, making creases at the corners of her mouth in a way she does when a man annoys her. At least, he notes, he's not the only one.

Phil takes the chicken platter from Eric and asks him, "You ordered the boat kit from Sweden?"

"Nooo," Eric says. He loves talking about his boat project. "Norway. Using the internet. I had tools and a big heated garage, so I thought, 'What the heck?' I work on it in the garage and my daughter helps." He whispers to Phil, "She's not here today."

"How long have you been building the boat?"

"KAYE! How long have I been in the garage with the boat?"

"Nine months."

"Bloody hell, it's a veritable gestation!"

"Ask him how far along he is," Kaye says to Phil.

"How far along?"

"Oh, not too." This is good, Eric thinks. No talk about Kaye's *detective work*. Sometimes Kaye's imagination is tiresome, and she won't be content with her own life. Then Eric notices Eugene watching his mother. She laughs at everything Phil says as if it is funny. Phil isn't really funny. Does Frank notice this? Of course he doesn't. Not after drinking so much.

Frank can never hold his liquor. Eugene's eyes flit between Eleanor and Phil. Eugene is young. He might not notice either. Poor lad, uncomfortable in his own skin.

Just as Phil compliments Eleanor on the chicken marinade, Eugene scowls and says, "We eat this all the time. It's nothing special."

Eric stops in the middle of drinking and speaks. "Lucky you then, Eugene! You have this all the time. It's delicious."

"It's not hard when you pour it from a jar," Eugene says. "She got it from the store."

Eleanor's face turns pink. "Since when have you paid attention? It's not from a bottle. It's homemade."

Eric catches Kaye whisper to her friend. "Too much house guest today?"

"It's in the way I grilled it!" Frank calls out. "That's the trick to good chicken."

"You aren't the greatest cook, Dad," Liam says, grinning.

A hum of uncomfortable laughter follows. Eleanor turns to Kaye and shrugs, then appeals to her son, "Liam!"

"At least he's honest. It's a good trait," Eric says to her.

Phil turns to Eugene and Liam. "My mother used to make everything from bottles and cans of processed foods, and she managed to make it all taste pretty good. At least, that's what I remember. She's no longer living. Really, it isn't a bad thing. But it's nice when your mom makes a little effort," he says. Eugene nods. Liam eats. Eleanor smiles briefly, thankfully.

Liam asks, "Are you drunk, Dad?"

Phil chuckles unexpectedly. Then the laughter stops. Eric has food in his mouth but feels strongly that he should say something. "It's not so terrible, son, to be drunk sometimes. Someday soon, Liam, you will also be drunk, for that is what young men do before they really grow up." Eric washes his food down with wine.

Surprised that his father isn't the one to answer, Liam's mouth falls open and he doesn't reply, as though he is caught in a single frame. Then Eric breaks into a smile and they all know that he is teasing Liam. Phil leans over and whispers something to Liam, who begins to appear relieved.

"Eric," says Kaye, "Leave the boy alone. He is being forced to eat dinner with boring adults. Give him a break." Then to Liam and Frank, "I think your father has had enough to drink, if that is what you mean."

"I was just asking. He's acting drunk," Liam says.

Eleanor laughs uncomfortably. "That's because he *is* drunk," she says.

Eric says, "Tell me, Phil, where exactly do you live?"

"An hour and a half west of Chicago."

"Now you can drink more because you aren't driving home," Frank holds up the bottle of wine.

"Dad!" Liam says.

Frank puts the bottle down. "No, no, I'm not drunk." He raises his eyebrows as he locks eyes with Eric and they both break into peals of laughter. Eric isn't sure why he is laughing. Phil looks to Eugene and smiles awkwardly. Eugene smiles back. Eric pours more wine. "Here, let's take care of this!"

"You are acting like children," Kaye says.

Eric steps out of his chair and throws his arms around her. He can feel her stiffness as he withdraws.

"Worse than children," Eugene says. "We're children and we don't act like they are acting."

"Well! I want to hear more about how Phil here knows the *lovely* Eleanor," Eric says.

"High school," Eleanor and Phil answer at the same time.

"Was she your girlfriend?" Liam asks.

"No. We were just friends." Phil winks.

"Your mother had no boyfriends until I came around," Frank says. "And to that I want to make a toast!" Frank raises his glass. "To my wife, who found me perfect and irresistible!" Raucous laughter from Eric and Frank pierces the air around the table. They raise their glasses, and Phil slowly follows suit. Kaye and Eleanor do not. Eric glances toward Eleanor. She looks mortified.

"I am going inside," Eugene tells his mother. "I've got a game to download. Is that okay, Mom?"

"I cannot believe he is so polite and asks," Eric says.

Eleanor nods. The boys take their plates inside. Frank is opening another bottle of wine. "Now we can say anything we want. The kids are gone," he says.

PHIL HAS HAD so much to drink that he is having trouble keeping his eyes open. He knows that he has dozed a couple of times. With the beer, the wine, the food, and the intensity of the evening, he has no energy left. It is as if he has been in hyperdrive and has come crashing down. Sarayu's call hovers in the back of his tired brain. He excuses himself and stands up. Eleanor touches his arm as he passes her.

He places a hand on her shoulder and smiles. "I need to move around." Eleanor turns to him and smiles as though she understands. At least, he thinks she does. She is being a good hostess and he hopes she hasn't noticed him nodding off. In the darkness he walks along the garden path to the alleyway, thinking that he is going unnoticed by everyone else. The dog, wandering in search of table scraps, follows him halfway down the path and growls before turning back.

As he stands at the back gate and the garage, Eleanor approaches him with a mug of coffee, the scent drifting toward him. She is not giving him much time to think about Sarayu, even though she doesn't know about her. But then, he knows he is here to see Eleanor. Sarayu shouldn't be part of the picture.

"Sorry, it's decaf," Eleanor says as he takes the coffee. "It's late. We're having dessert. Want to join us?"

THE DINNER PARTY is over. After helping to do the dishes, Kaye and Eric have left, and Frank and Eleanor have gone to bed. Phil can hear their sons beyond his closed bedroom door, in the hallway, the younger one talking through the bathroom door to his brother inside. Phil holds his phone in his hand, trying to decide if he should call Sarayu. He dials and relishes listening to her voice on her voice mail. When she asks for a message, he hesitates. He is so tired. He has had too much to drink. He is anxious about what to say. "Oh . . . Sarayu," he breathes out against the phone, and then realizes that this is the message he has recorded.

He opens the window and sits on the bed, watching the curtain float in the darkness. He hears children from a distant backyard, awake and outside playing, late. Then a barking dog. He feels almost hopeful that Sarayu will forgive him because he will explain that he didn't know how she felt about him—about how he felt about her—and he feels that he now knows. This will happen and Eleanor won't think that he is a bad person, and he can move on with his divorce. His life.

He is seeing the consequences of what he has done. He aches at his wife's tunnel vision, that she did not understand what would happen to him when the physical part of their marriage ended, that her religion, her new boyfriend (he has never before dared to call this guy a "boyfriend") had made him desperate for the part of a relationship where you touch someone and experience intimacy. The postcoital closeness that he felt when she rested her head in the crook of his arm, her long hair tickling his chest and chin, his shoulder. This was something Sarayu provided generously. He checks his phone again. Nothing. Then he gets into bed, his head buzzing with exhaustion. He climbs under the blanket and waits. *Please, Eleanor, don't think I'm a bad person.*

14

LYING IN BED, Eleanor tries to make sense of the evening. She can't sleep. She replays the scenes in her head. She wonders what Phil is thinking of her husband's drunkenness, of her sons' belligerence, of the fact that this, her family, her body of work, isn't all that she had described it to be. She wonders how people do internet dating, when you can just lie and lie about yourself. How do they maintain the lies?

If she could summon some of Kaye's courage, she would knock on his door.

But it would be a tremendous act of desperation. Was she desperate to get him to like her—to be attracted to her? How long can you flirt with someone over the airwaves, sharing personal bits of your life as if the person you are communicating with is the only person you share with?

She can hear Phil's door close from where she sits on her bed. Frank is in a drunken sleep. The boys are in their rooms, probably awake, probably communicating with each other by texting and using handheld gaming devices and headphones. Eleanor recalls a time when Eugene, as a little boy, went to visit his dad's office on Take Your Children to Work Day, and was shocked that his father spoke to his colleagues in the adjacent offices via email, rather than simply walking next door.

What if the boys knew what she was thinking? They wouldn't. They couldn't.

Eleanor listens for more from next door in Phil's room, but the low hum of the ceiling fan blocks out small noises. Annie lies on the floor, curled up next to the bed. She pops her head up, ears pricked as if she knows what Eleanor is thinking, and she prepares to follow her. She sits up, puts her paw on the bed. Eleanor scratches her forehead and Annie settles down again and closes her eyes. Eleanor puts on her robe, leaves the room, and softly closes the door behind her.

She taps Phil's door quietly. Phil says to come in. With her head in the space of the open door, she asks, "Everything ok? The temperature? Do you have enough towels?"

Phil looks up from his phone. He is bare-chested with the quilt up high over his stomach, leaning against the headboard, the reading light on. He smiles sadly, says "Everything is fine," and looks at her as though there might be something else to say. She hesitates and can't help but glance again at the pale, firm skin of his chest, before closing the door.

Frank is almost awake when she returns to bed. "What's up?" he asks sleepily.

"Checking on the boys."

He reaches for her under the blanket. It's the last thing she wants right now.

"We have a houseguest in the next room," she says. "It isn't on my mind."

Frank passes out again, curled around her. He won't remember this. She can feel the weight of his body relax and become heavy just as she tenses more. His head is on her shoulder, his arm on her belly, his leg over her thigh as he slips into an oppressive sleep. His body is very warm and his skin sweats onto hers. She can smell the alcohol and the sour sweat. She tries to move his body parts without making him stir. In the next room, Phil's bed squeaks, his door closes. He is walking down the steps. Eventually she can feel the house adjust as the front door opens. What is he doing? She tries to stay where she is. He could be doing anything, getting something from his car, even leaving. Annie barks once. Frank doesn't waken. The dog makes a noisy circle before settling into a ball of fur beside the bed. Eleanor looks out into the dark. When she doesn't hear the sound of Phil climbing back up the stairs, she gets up gently, quietly, puts on a pair of shorts and a T-shirt, and creeps out of the bedroom.

PHIL IS SITTING under the roof overhang on the top step of the front porch. It is raining lightly and his long, bare feet glisten with small drops of rain. He turns as Eleanor opens the screen door and smiles. "Do you want the light? You can't see a thing out here."

"No." He pats the space next to him.

"You're getting wet," Eleanor says as she sits down there.

He has an embarrassed smile. "I like the rain." He leans back and stretches his neck. "I had a good time tonight."

"Really?' She moves to the side and they brush arms. "Some night."

"Yes." He laughs. "That Kaye . . ."

Eleanor nods. She looks out past the dark walkway to the grass and street, lit dimly by the city's historical street lamps.

Cars are parked intermittently along the curb. The rain makes a soft pattering noise on the roof and the walk and canopy of tree leaves that arches over it, steady and calming.

"I came out here for fresh air," he says. "I couldn't fall asleep."

"Me neither. Is the air conditioning too cold inside?"

"No, Eleanor. Everything is fine. Everything in your house and your family and friends are fine. Honestly, I'm jealous." He smiles and places a hand on her wrist and squeezes gently. "I have a lot on my plate," he says.

"The divorce?"

"Not just." He looks down at the steps. "You know that woman I had the affair with?"

"Yes." Eleanor's mood drops.

"She called and left me a message this evening." He puts his hands together and raises his head and then looks down, but his hand moves back on top of hers. He doesn't look at her, but she watches his profile carefully. "I don't want you to think I'm a bad person."

"I don't! I don't think you are a bad person." In the faint light from the doorway behind them, she can see that his eyes are steady and wide, and his mouth is flat. He turns to see her. His face begs her to say that this is more than his being a good or bad person. He is someone who makes mistakes, she thinks.

"I don't think you are a bad person." She puts her arm around his stiff shoulders, which loosen as she draws him closer. His breath is on the nape of her neck. "Just complicated." Eleanor feels a line of moisture move down the inside of her thigh. Funny how comforting Phil can make her think about sex. It is never that way with Frank. "Everyone has doubts about marriage. There are moments we all want to stray. Marriage and sex are complicated." She smiles.

She moves against him and he moves with her. Their lips press, their teeth collide as he attempts to open her mouth further with his tongue. And then she has the feeling of a warm wave overcoming her. He stops. "Don't think badly of me," he whispers, but she takes his mouth again, guiding his chin with the tips of her fingers, and then pushes against him.

"I don't," she says.

"THAT'S IT?"

Eleanor knows that what she has just said is the wrong thing. But she is thinking about the unsatisfied ache between her thighs and all the trouble she has gone through to be here to try to satisfy that ache. She and Phil are both lying on an old, crusty blanket that she found in the car trunk and put on the cracked cement floor of her garage. She is frustrated, disappointed, and uncomfortable. They are *naked,* and he is *limp.*

"I'm sorry," he says to her. "Maybe this just isn't meant to be. It's probably better that it didn't work out. I don't want to hurt anyone. Not anyone else."

Eleanor is struck by the fact that, though the garage is very dark, the floor is cold and it smells like gasoline, and they can't see much of each other, Phil is not acting very embarrassed while humiliation is seeping into her consciousness. Eleanor can feel her family steps away. They are so close to the house. And still naked.

He touches her elbow and a shot of electricity shoots through her. *Should we try again?* No. *Relief, nothing really happened.* She begins to calm down. *Again, relief. No penetration. Nothing really happened.*

"Look," Phil says, sitting up and reaching for his clothes. "We could try this again some other time if you want. But in reality, this sort of sneaking around isn't a good idea. Look at all you have, your husband, your kids. I don't want to ruin that."

Relief. And now she is feeling limp herself. *Guilty, guilty. But nothing really happened.* She tells herself this, in her head. Maybe, in the end, it doesn't matter if she wanted it to. Or, if she tried. The end result was that nothing happened. *Nothing but residual embarrassment.*

She wants her own soft bed. But first she wants to shower. She gets up off of the grinding concrete, and in a thin stream of light from the window, she sees Phil smile at her. She begins to put on her clothes and pick up the dirty blanket. *Why hadn't she suggested that she be on top?* No. Definitely she had not thought this through. Or, perhaps, she had thought too much about it and not at all about what a stupid idea it was. She opens the garage door quietly and peers out onto the dark yard. They walk silently to the back door, one after the other. Eleanor goes to the basement, to an old shower no one uses anymore, and washes off the night.

15

"I **KNOW WHO** you are. And I am sure you know who I am."

Sarayu read the email. She knew who it came from. Sarayu read it, and it stayed in her head, brought back the guilt and the sadness she had suppressed after the affair ended.

Sarayu's anger flared at Linda's attempt to intimidate; it made her want to confront Linda, in person.

So, on a bitter morning, Sarayu packed a sandwich and a thermos of coffee and drove out of the city, weaving through the streets to the expressway. She passed the long stretches of industry, block-like windowless buildings and wide parking lots crammed with cars, one factory or warehouse after another. And then, along the expressway, the populated area morphed into office building groupings with sculpted lawns. Eventually, farms stretched along the sides of the road as she got closer to where Phil lived.

"I know how you feel hearing from me," Linda had written. "I have faced his infidelity before. Now, I want to move on. I am not doing this for you. I am doing this for me."

Past the billboards advertising state-line casinos and ambulance chasers, she came to Phil's small riverside town.

The trees along the river road were bare, the sky an empty grey. She held her breath and let it go slowly, then repeated the process, hardly recognizing that she was doing it.

SARAYU REPLAYED THE email in her head and tried to map out what she would say to Linda. As she turned on to the gravel street of Phil and Linda's development, she was sure that Phil would not be there.

Her anger sparked again as she came to the beginning of their block, where she could see their empty driveway ahead. She turned onto the street and parked across from Phil's house. She sat for a moment, unsure. She could still back away from the confrontation. But what satisfaction would that give her? The house looked empty, no movement beyond the open curtains. She got out of the car.

Sarayu walked up to the house and around to the side, then came to the path leading to the front door, where she heard and saw the door open.

In that small moment, she was struck with the fear of being caught. What if it was Phil?

Nothing came to her mind. She knew she was not a good liar. As she stood still, an arm emerged to push the outer door, then a thin, tall body, and finally a blonde fifteen-year-old girl closed the door behind her and stopped short when she saw Sarayu.

The girl didn't speak. It was the middle of the day, and she should have been in school. The lit cigarette in the girl's hand made Sarayu sure that neither Phil nor Linda were at home.

The two of them looked at each other, caught in their

individual crimes.

"Hi," the girl said, straightening the shoulder strap of her book bag. "Who are you?"

"I'm—I'm an old friend of your father's."

"He's not home right now."

"Ah." Sarayu smiled at the girl, who did not return the look. "Then I should come back when he is." She turned toward her car and began to walk slowly, the energy in her body draining with each step. Then she stopped and turned back to the girl, who was still standing on the path, holding her cigarette and her book bag, watching Sarayu.

"What is your name? I'll tell him you were here."

"You must have a day off from school," Sarayu said. "My name is Anna. Tell him—tell your mom, too—that I came by."

The girl looked puzzled and spread her lips into a smile, revealing a mouth filled with metal braces. "Sure," she said.

"Thanks."

Sarayu got into her car with confidence. The girl wouldn't say a word to either parent about the strange woman on the walkway.

16

MONDAY MORNING: ELEANOR has spent the night awake or dozing, and having brief, frightening dreams in which Frank walks in on her while she is having sex with Phil (not just trying to have sex with Phil). The dreams take place in different rooms in Eleanor's house, but not the garage. When she wakes, she has the feeling of not sleeping, and at the same time, of having done something horribly bad.

When Frank comes into the kitchen to say to her that he is leaving for work, she jumps in her chair. "Touchy!" he says. "Maybe you should go out and walk the dog."

She looks up at him and he gives her a sideways hug. "You aren't still angry that I got drunk with Eric the other night, when your friend was visiting?" He gently takes her chin with two fingers and turns it toward him. She thinks, he really is so clueless. But do people ever believe things they don't want to believe? "Please don't be. It doesn't happen very often. Maybe I was jealous that you invited a guy from high school to our home. I mean, it isn't that I worry about making any sort of impression on that guy. What a drip." He kisses her cheek.

"No, that's over with," she says. "He was a drip. I'm tired."

"It really was one of the worst dinner parties we have ever had."

She can tell that he is trying to make her laugh, but she can't.

He casts a suspicious look at her, at least that is how she interprets it, and then leaves. In her chair at the kitchen island, she tries desperately not to think about what happened on the porch to turn her on to Phil so much.

But trying not to think about it makes her think about it. She never wants to see or hear from him again. Saturday morning, he was in her home. As she and Phil had planned, she woke early to see him off, started the coffee maker, sliced bagels she had purchased specially from an old New York bagel maker on Dempster, waited nervously for Phil to come downstairs before anyone else arose. At the top of the landing, looking into the kitchen, he stood for a moment and she watched the pale blue eyes that she found still stirred her. She felt mixed up. He broke into a smile and opened his arms as he walked down the stairs. "Come on, it isn't all that bad." No other man she knew would ever act this way.

What wasn't bad, she thought? The shared intimacy? The fact that he couldn't get it up? The amount of alcohol they'd drunk? The fact that they were in *her* home, *her* garage?

But she did not want a prolonged discussion. She wanted him to leave so that she could begin to forget the whole thing, and yet she was afraid to let him go and be left with the creepy fact that they had attempted intercourse in her garage.

"You okay about last night?" Phil said. "I don't want us to be on bad terms."

She lied, "Neither do I," but wasn't sure her body language followed what she was telling him. "What time are you seeing your daughter?" Her attempt to change the subject.

"A little later. But I know you want me out of here. And that's okay." He sat down and poured his own coffee.

They drank quietly and ate bagels. Eleanor said nothing, though things were racing through her mind. *Why did you let me try to have sex with you here? Why did we do all of this while my family was home? While the neighbors were next door, while my sons were asleep in their rooms? So, you could come into a place where you weren't known and leave a mess behind you? Go. Go and don't come back.*

Then, finally, he received a text, looked at his phone, then at her, and said it was time to leave. "It's my daughter. She's awake early."

Eleanor looked at him. In the end she did not want to confront him. She just wanted him to go.

Now, on Monday morning, as she sits in her kitchen, she wonders how Phil came to be the way he is, a jerk, something she thought she might understand because of the vague way she remembered him in high school, and how she thought he might be the answer to the boredom in her life. And now she has the guilt that she is going to have to haul around for a while. Maybe forever. It seems like forever right now. But at least she doesn't ever have to speak to Phil again.

Eugene leaves the front door wide open as he bounds down the steps to the sidewalk on his large, floppy feet, arms flailing as he attempts to catch the bus to the high school. Liam has another twenty minutes before he leaves. He makes his own lunch and packs his backpack. "What the heck is wrong with you?" he asks his mother. She merely looks at him. The radio is on loudly and Liam turns it off. Usually she tells him to leave it alone so that she can hear the news, but she hardly notices.

"Eugene left the front door open," he complains.

"Hmm."

"He does half as many chores as I do. Why do I have to close the door he leaves open?"

"Did I ask you to?"

"You were about to."

Then, looking puzzled, he walks away. He has left dishes and food on the counter for her to see. Eleanor snaps to. "Put them in the dishwasher," she calls to him. She sees his head around the corner of the doorway.

"Why should I have to put dishes in the dishwasher when Eugene doesn't? Answer me, Mom. I am asking you why?" "Because you are a better person." She doesn't even know why she is saying this but she is not in the mood for an argument. Something is telling her that she should be doing everything for this kid so that he can grow up thinking his mother loves him, that she is not the type of person to ignore him. Another voice is telling her to come out of herself and her self-loathing and be a regular mom. "You are here," she says. "So put your dishes in the dishwasher. When you are three years older, Eugene's age, have a huge amount of high school homework, and puberty and your grossly underdeveloped frontal lobe make you forget everything, we will revisit the issue of your chores. For now, you do as I say."

Liam does it and stomps off. There are days, Eleanor thinks, as she locks the front door behind him, that she wishes her children would speak to her in texted partial words and partial sentences, because today Liam has too many words, and each one reminds her of how shitty she feels for almost doing something horrible.

Eleanor takes a package of Italian sausages out of the freezer for dinner, runs water into a pan, and puts the package into it to defrost. She doesn't want to think about tonight's dinner or anything else, so she leaves it and turns to the ping of her phone, where there is an email from Phil's wife.

Eleanor doesn't have the sense or lack of curiosity to ignore it. "Eleanor," the email reads, "I know my husband was with you this past weekend," she writes. "He still tells me everything. I don't know why he wants to be honest with me now, after all of his lies. Maybe he is afraid I might smell something on him? After all, he knows I don't trust him."

Eleanor blinks. She would pinch herself if it wasn't corny. She wants to write, "Really? REALLY? Why should you care? What are you still doing living in his house while you are seeing another guy? What makes you such a martyr?"

But that would only fire Linda up, and the conversation would go on forever. No. It is time to get out of this mess, Eleanor thinks. She imagines Linda's face, and it makes her angry, the weakness in Linda's expressions, her soft compliant voice. "I am sorry you are upset," Eleanor writes. "What makes you think he isn't lying this time? Do you always smell his clothes when he comes home from anywhere? Why would you assume it was me?" She deletes it all. "He was here," she writes. "We had a family weekend. My husband joined us, as well as another couple, and my sons. We barbecued." What normal woman sleeps with her houseguest while her husband is home? She presses send.

Linda's answer is fast: "I knew he wasn't with the last woman he had an affair with. The nurse. I emailed her on Friday to say that Phil is leaving me. She said that he wasn't there." Eleanor finds it odd that Linda is so trusting of people who lie.

Linda continues: "Did he say I was leaving him?"

"You told me."

"We are sorting through the property now. Ultimately we will divorce."

Eleanor compares this with what she heard from Phil, the stories of sitting at the dining room table with papers that represented their lives together, the kind of thing Frank might do with her if he knew what had happened in the garage. Eleanor can now replace her guilt with Linda's drama, which seems to suck the anxiety right out of her. "Why did you contact this other woman?" she types. "Isn't it over?" Does she mean Linda and Phil, or Phil and the other woman?

Linda could be laughing now at the absurdity of all this, if Linda were normal—and Eleanor is thinking that Linda is not.

"Not for her," Linda writes back. "Now that he is almost free. And she wasn't the only one. There was another one before her. That I know about. Then when he was in the military, who even knows about that? I had no control over him. He was in another country. Prostitutes. Parties. Who knows? I never asked for details. I got credit card bills for rooms. What an idiot he was. I thought it was all part of being a marine's wife. I was so young. Maybe he was the kind of guy who just couldn't go without sex for six months, and it got me off the hook when he came home."

If only she knew how he'd flopped over the weekend.

And now you can control who he is with next by contacting his former lover? How does that work? Eleanor thinks. "I don't believe you," she writes. But of course, she does. It gives her someone else to blame for what she has done. "This isn't the boy I remember from high school. He was going with the same girl for two years, junior and senior year. They even stayed together for part of college."

"I didn't know him then."

At this point Eleanor isn't sure where the conversation is going, and she is fraught with anxiety, though her curiosity is still strong. "You are making up the story about the marines. I can't believe he would do that"—actually she can, she does, but she doesn't want Linda to suspect this. "He doesn't at all seem the type. He seems quiet. Like he doesn't get out much"—which she knows he does, otherwise what would he be doing at her house, in her garage?

"Are you drunk? Why are you doing this?" Eleanor begins to write some more, then she cancels. She looks up as if someone is there to distract her. But it is only the dog, who trots to the back door and barks to be let out. Eleanor writes, "I'm not out to get you. Honestly. I was just a person curious about a boy I went to high school with."

"No matter," Linda responds. "I'm a Christian. I've been saved by Jesus Christ. I'm concerned for your soul, for you getting mixed up with this man. He leaves a trail of women behind him. Look at me. I'm one of them."

Eleanor reads this twice. Linda is angry, mischievous, probably bored and writing all of this to pass the time, a distraught almost-ex-wife who has no control over what her husband does. After the last series of emails, where Linda claimed to want to save Eleanor's soul, Eleanor finds all of this troubling. If Eleanor reacts angrily, then Linda will win some satisfaction in this ridiculous battle of emails, she will have achieved a purpose. So, to counteract this, she writes back: "I am just trying to live my life here. I believe Phil told

WE HAVE EVERYTHING BEFORE US

me about his situation with you because I don't live in your town. I am a voice with no face even though he knew me in high school and came to my home for dinner one time. I might have answered things in emails that were intended to comfort him through his marriage breakup, and you took them the wrong way." Saying something like this smooths over some of Eleanor's guilt, in the same way an apology to someone who doesn't deserve one does. "I am not doing anything at all that would affect your marriage." *Broken marriage.* "Or your divorce. I don't wish bad things on you." *No. Truthfully, I just wish you would vanish.*

There is a break. Eleanor puts on the kettle, then she hears a ping from her phone. "Tell me more about the weekend," Linda writes.

But at this point Eleanor is confident that she has the upper hand and that Linda's messages have the undertone of a woman trying to cling to a man as he runs away, and she doesn't want to continue. It only reminds her of her own sins and makes her feel like crap. So, she dials Kaye.

"What the heck is she emailing you for?" Kaye screams into the phone.

"I don't know. She thinks something went on in my house during the visit." This exits her mouth so quickly that she immediately regrets that she has said it. (She wants to let it out to someone. To Kaye.) Then she breathes deeply and lets the air flow out in a slow stream. She tells herself that she can learn how to lie well. "Mostly she wants to tell me what a horrible person he is."

"Is he such a horrible person?" Kaye asks, and Eleanor interprets it as a query: did something happen on Phil's visit? "He seemed a little clueless, but better than the last time."

"Just because he believed you when you said you were a cop . . ."

"I'm going to come up with a new story for the next time we go clubbing with your ex-boyfriends and their ex-wives."

"Something about this woman—it's as if she is talking to a therapist—she is not a woman who really knows her husband. She's putting out feelers to find out what he is doing. She doesn't know me at all. Or whether to trust what I say."

"But she is praying for you." Kaye makes a snorting sound, laughter.

"God." Eleanor looks out the back open window and watches the house sparrows pick things up from the ground near the trash bins, labels that have fallen out of the garbage bags, puffs of dog undercoat, twigs, they make a trajectory upward toward the eaves.

"There has got to be a reason why you want to hang out with this guy. Look at him: he's attractive if you like that buffed, Scandinavian, former-military look. Frankly, I don't care if anything did or is going to happen between you. Just be careful. The emails from his wife are weird. Even dangerous. You don't know her. She still lives with him even though he says they are getting a divorce and it is her idea to leave. He comes to your home and *she* wants to know the details of the whole affair or whatever you want to call it. The list goes on. If she found your emails on his computer, she can find your house. She can find Frank and she can call him at work. What will happen then?"

"None of that will happen," Eleanor says, but she doesn't believe her own words and it frightens her. She looks for excuses. "Other than what she writes, she seemed like a reserved person when we met her. The type who starves herself to make a point about her own suffering. She doesn't seem aggressive."

"You don't know her. She is writing to you. You are like an old girlfriend from high school and she cares. That, to me, is aggressive behavior. Have you ever initiated the emails?"

"No."

"Are you sure it's even her writing those emails?"

Eleanor stands at the sink and looks out the window at the wire fence and the spindly bushes and fluttering green leaves that divide her property from the neighbor's. She pours her tea down the drain. "You are right," she says.

After dislodging herself from Kaye, she follows the sparrows upstairs and sits on her bed, staring out the double glass doors of the balcony as the birds flit back and forth, making their homes with the foraged material in their beaks. She is in a situation, she thinks, and she can't/won't be able to find a way to feel better about it. Out on the balcony, she stands and looks up at the sparrows. They hop and fly around the pigeon spikes, stabbing twigs into the pile of garbage that is their nest. Eleanor picks up the broom. She pulls out a wooden chair and climbs on it, swats, reaching the spikes, sending the sparrows out and upward and away. "Stop!" she screams at them. "Go away!" She slaps and slaps at the twigs and fur and cigarette butts, and they all fall to the ground below, just as the chair tips and Eleanor finds herself sprawled and weeping on the wooden slats of the balcony floor.

17

THE HOUSE IS empty again. Phil stands in the kitchen with his phone to his ear. In the background he can hear the sounds of the outdoors, wind rustling the grasses in the field beyond his property, robins calling out, neighbors talking to their children, all through the open windows and doors. He has waited all day to call Sarayu back, sitting at work, distracted, unable to concentrate. His wife at her desk, ten feet away. She made comments about how he wasn't paying attention. And now, standing over the kitchen sink, looking out the window, watching Phoenix investigate the backyard, he listens to the rings of Sarayu's line and for a moment he thinks of Eleanor.

He paces. What a fuck up at her house. He takes a sponge from the sink basin and wipes the table, the countertops, the island, trying to clean things up. He disowns his embarrassment. If he spends too much time thinking about what happened with Eleanor . . . He feels he got out of the situation ok. He straightens the chairs around the table. "It's Phil," he says to the electronic voice on Sarayu's voicemail. "Still playing phone tag. Looking forward to talking to you."

If he were to spend every day dwelling on all of his mistakes, he would be unable to move forward, to move away from his troubles with Linda. Sarayu seems to want to be friends again. He can concentrate on fixing what happened with her, at least for now. The rest—Linda, and perhaps Eleanor—he must put behind him.

Phoenix is at the door waiting to come in. He scoops kibble into her bowl and she pants as she crosses the threshold before digging into her food with her nose. She looks up at Phil for more as he picks up his phone to dial again.

This time she is there, a deeply feminine voice answers as if she is asking a question, because, Phil thinks, she knows he is the one calling. He hesitates because he doesn't know what to say. He may have thought about it all weekend, on the drive home, and at work today. But now his mind is blank. There is nothing he can do to make up for the email he sent to her breaking off their affair.

"Sarayu?"

"Yes? Phil?"

He hesitates again. "How are you?"

Another open space in the conversation, and he fears it will be filled with one-word answers and long, long gaps. "You called a couple of days ago. Is everything okay?"

"Is everything okay?" she asks, quietly. "Yes. What about you?"

"Same old," he answers. For now, he wants to say that he wants his wife to find a new place for herself, that the divorce was her idea, that he had really tried to be faithful to Linda after Sarayu. Yet he also wants to say that he made a mistake when he said that he didn't want to see her again. Again, he imagines the smooth skin of her cheek and the fringe of her black hair falling over her forehead, and he feels a strong long-ing for her that covers up, or acts as a palliative, for the events of the weekend. "No. That isn't what I meant to say," comes out of his mouth.

"No?" she says.

"No."

"Divorce?"

"Yes."

"From what you have told me in the past, your wife would not have stayed with you. Not by now."

"No."

Another space.

"I have a new job," she says. "I'm in Chicago at a local hospital. It wasn't hard to find. Every hospital needs nurses."

He laughs uncomfortably.

"Same apartment," she says. "You have only been here once. Maybe you don't remember it."

"Of course I remember it."

In the quiet he can hear her breathing, or perhaps he imagines it. And he thinks of her sitting at her window in the soft chair where they had once sat together, she curled into his body in the early morning after they had been awake all night, and the sun shone lightly through the summer leaves into the apartment. He breathes deeply and wonders if he will ever feel that sense of peace and romance again. Then some-thing unexpected comes out—"Can I see you?"—when what he should actually have said is that he is sorry for hurting her, but the words jumble.

"No," she says with immediacy. "Not now, but we can talk on the phone." He can hear the rush of air that comes from her speaking against the phone, powerful and brief.

"Would that be all right with you?"

"Yes." He wants to see her face and what sort of expression she has on it. "I am so sorry, Sarayu," he finally says. "Don't be angry with me. Don't hate me."

"I don't hate you."

"It was what it was."

"No. It's not like that at all," she says, and he can sense her sadness, unless it is his own. "Listen, I need to get somewhere. I have to go. But we can talk again. Can't we? You have my number. I have yours. I promise that we will talk again. All right?"

He feels himself nod. "I'm sorry. I'm so sorry."

"Yes," she says. "I hope so."

"We'll talk soon, if that is okay with you."

"Soon is fine."

When they have said their goodbyes, simple, one-word exits, he sits on the floor of his kitchen and puts his hand on Phoenix's paw. She tolerates this. It is difficult for him to sort out what is going on in his head right now. That Sarayu had called him. That she wanted to talk to him again. He is emotionally spent, he thinks, but it's more than that. He looks around at all of his wife's belongings, shoes under the table, a sweater on the back of a chair. All of it unwanted. It won't be her house in the end, yet she has marked her territory. Now, this minute, he wants the divorce finalized, and this is a thought he would like to share with someone, like Eleanor, but he has ruined that relationship.

He is reluctant to communicate with Eleanor—should he apologize? The entire incident did not seem to be one person's fault. How did things get so complicated? How did they get to the garage in her house? There is so much in his head right now that it is difficult to feel a single emotion, like embarrassment. He was tired, not at all alert. He fell into the situation with Eleanor—he was drunk—then, with the call from Sarayu on his mind, he could not perform. This hadn't happened in a long time, certainly not with Sarayu. Eleanor seemed like the kind of woman who would understand. But that was not how she had reacted. And he really did not want that sort of relationship with her, the kind where she cheats on her husband with him. He never did. So, could they go back to being friends? Could he write to her? Would she write back? And would she tell her husband about what happened?

If he were writing to her, if he was sure she wasn't angry with him, he would tell her, "I want my life sorted out. I want to move on. I want my wife to pack her things and take all of the junk she has left all over the house. This was all her idea: leaving me. Why can't she just get it together and move out?"

But he is not writing to Eleanor. He will not. On the floor of the kitchen, petting the dog, he breathes so deeply that he feels he will explode in tears. Still, he does nothing. He is not writing to anyone on the computer, or throwing a chair, or shouting. Phoenix looks up into his eyes with an ignorance of what sort of person he has been. To her, he could be an ax murderer, he thinks, and then laughs out loud at his own joke. "Hey girl," he says to his dog.

Phoenix gives him some hope. She makes few demands. She loves to be petted. She puts her head on his lap, and, in a way, he feels some relief and a tiny bit of happiness. Sarayu does not hate him after what he has done to her. There will be another call, something he can look forward to. *Another call.* He leans back against the painted wall, which is cool to the touch, and closes his eyes. "She doesn't hate me," he says to himself. Two other women may hate him, Linda and Eleanor, but Sarayu does not. In the quiet of the kitchen, before his wife and daughter come home for the evening, he feels his lips spread into a smile.

PHIL IS IN bed reading when Linda and their youngest daughter come home. They enter the house with excited voices and Phil, at first, thinks that they are chatting; when he listens more carefully, he realizes that they are arguing. He laughs to himself that Linda is dealing with whatever this is alone. He hears the crinkle of plastic shopping bags. They must have been to the mall. At least it wasn't church, he thinks, or maybe it was both.

They come into the house as if he doesn't live here anymore. They go to the kitchen and he hears the door of the refrigerator open.

He hears his wife's light footsteps on the carpeted stairs, then a tap on the door to the bedroom.

"What is it?" He puts his book on the bedside table and watches her peek through the door.

"I need to talk to you?" She says it like she is asking rather than demanding.

"I'm here," he answers. She has always put things in the form of a question, something he thought was an element of being shy. Now he believes it is a part of the passive-aggressive behavior associated with their split up. There always seems to be something she has planned beneath the artificial question.

"I'm here," he says, again.

She walks into the room. Where she once would have sat

ESTHER YIN-LING SPODEK

near him on the bed in this situation, she stands near the doorway. "I spoke to the real estate agent today. I'm putting an offer on a new place."

He smiles without thinking about it, then says, "Why so soon?"

"That's not nice, Phil."

He shrugs. "You told me you wanted to leave me months ago. You are still here."

She shields her forehead with the palm of her hand and looks down at the floor. To him, in this moment, she looks frail. "It's not my fault," she says.

"I know."

"I guess that's it." She turns around.

"Wait." He dislikes calling her name.

"What?"

"Where is the house?"

"It's a ten-minute drive from here. Isabel can go back and forth."

"Where did you take her this evening?"

"Shopping. She wanted to go to the mall."

"You could have let me know."

She is facing the door. "Why? It was a last-minute thing."

"But it's a forty-five-minute drive each way. And it's almost ten on a school night."

She turns to look at him. "Yes." She walks out the door and closes it softly behind her.

Phil returns to his book. This time it is a novel that Eleanor had recommended and loaned to him. He can't concentrate on it. He thinks of the conversation with his wife, how he feels she controls it. He thinks of Sarayu and their phone call and imagines other telephone conversations, strangely similar conversations to the emails he had exchanged with Eleanor. In his imagination, Sarayu tells him about the commute to her new job in Chicago, the el and a bus, what her neighborhood is like in the summer—and what she does every day. He thinks of her rising in the morning, swinging her brown legs over the side of the bed and sliding her delicate narrow feet into slippers. He sees her padding in her nightgown to the kitchen to make coffee, reaching into the cabinet for the filters and a mug. He remembers her kitchen, the painted white cabinets, metal countertops, and light green walls. It was a place where she had not spent a lot of time because her job took her away too much. All of this distracts him from his wife and her behavior. Just as Sarayu had in the past. Just as Eleanor had for a while. He wants to call, email, text Sarayu, but consciously he is going to be careful with her now, take it slowly. He wants to ask her what she is doing and picture it. This might settle him into sleep.

Instead, Phil gets out of bed and walks to the door. He hears Linda and Isabel talking in the kitchen. They laugh as they talk (he hopes it isn't about him). This echoes through the family room and the hallway to the stairs, like an old, old sound he isn't used to anymore. He reaches for his T-shirt and shorts and dresses to go downstairs. As he approaches the kitchen, he calls out their names and they stop talking. "So, you went to the mall," he says. Linda nods and leaves as soon as he enters the room.

"Hi, Dad," Isabel says. Where she used to stop what she was doing and throw her arms around his neck, here she merely turns from halfway inside the refrigerator. He isn't sure if it's the breakup of her parents' marriage or adolescence that makes her act this way. He walks to her and kisses her cheek.

"You going to show me what you bought?"

Isabel leaves the refrigerator and lifts the shopping bag up to the countertop. She lays out the clothing she has purchased: a bathing suit, shorts, T-shirts, all in bright colors. He looks over these items, sees the price tags, and smiles because it is all more expensive than he feels it should be.

Then, this is the instant when it dawns on him that he will soon no longer have these occasions. He won't be waiting up for his wife and daughter, and he won't be able to hold on to the family moments. They are already gone. He hugs and kisses his daughter good night and reminds her to let the dog out. He passes the guest room—now his wife's room—on the way to the stairs. His wife is locked in for the night.

IN THE OFFICE, on Thursday, Carol, an administrative assistant, brings homemade coffee cake. Phil eats three large slices, one after the other, which is not part of his diet, but he can't help himself. This makes Carol happy, and the other gals tease him that stress is going to fatten him up. Linda is nowhere to be seen today. She is, perhaps, taking a personal day. Since she is co-owner of the company, she can do this, but she has yet to call in.

After two local sales calls, Phil sits at his computer, taking a break. He has not written to Eleanor since seeing her almost a week ago. She has not written to him. He now believes that he should not burn bridges. And to show that this is true, at least for him, he opens up his account and begins to write to her.

"Dear Eleanor," he starts. "I made it home okay. The weather was good. The roads were good. No traffic. Came home to an empty house. Don't know where everyone was, maybe at church. They go to church a lot these days. It keeps Linda busy and out of my hair.

"Lunch with my daughter was good. She has a couple of exams coming up, and school doesn't end until June, so she is a little stressed.

"I really appreciate that you invited me for dinner. I don't get invited to dinner much. Linda took all of our friends, so my social life, you know, is limited. They are on her side. They see me at the supermarket or the gas station and shoot looks at me like I've done something terrible to them. I know I haven't hurt them personally.

"I hope I haven't caused any trouble between you and Frank. I think he's a nice guy. And I am sorry things didn't work like we had hoped. I like you a lot. I would like us to be friends, even if the situation is awkward.

"Think it over. I still want to be your friend. I'm still here."

He hesitates before he presses send. He glances to see if any of the other people in the office can see him.

No one in the office will know.

18

SARAYU WALKS QUICKLY along a street perpendicular to her own, crowded with people looking into the windows of shops and those exiting from the el stop ahead. She checks her wallet again. She wouldn't want Phil to pay for her dinner. She is done with that. She walks anxiously along a block of ethnic restaurants, Turkish, Italian, Asian, coffee and frozen yogurt, a couple of taquerias, all reflecting the people moving in and out of the neighborhood. Once, Scandinavian immigrants dominated, but the last Swedish bakery has closed.

Sarayu wants to get to the restaurant—she can't help rushing—but she doesn't want to be early. Phil is frequently on time, and she wants him to wait. It's been two weeks since his wife, Linda, emailed Sarayu to tell her about the divorce, and to ask if Phil was with her. Of course he wasn't with her. The email was a shock. "I know all about you," Linda wrote.

Why did Sarayu open the email this time? Was it the heading, "a message from Phil Anderson's wife?" Why do people open emails that should be left alone? Are they so easily manipulated by their inane curiosity, the reason why they get caught up in email scams and send money they will never see again? She had never seen herself that way.

"Is he with you? We are getting a divorce, which, of course, is partially your fault. It's his fault too. Is he with you? I'm praying for both of you, for you are both sinners and you will get your just desserts."

Sarayu did not believe the mumbo jumbo of Linda's judgmental Christianity. She did not believe in paying for your sins. She was doing nothing with Phil. But she did believe that they were getting a divorce.

"Please do not contact me again," she wrote in return to Linda's email. She wanted to tell her to fuck off, but as a medical professional, she knew it wasn't a good idea to antagonize someone who is crazy.

Now she was going to meet Phil for dinner. She took hours deciding what to wear. She did her makeup, washed it off, and did it again. She had picked the date and the restaurant. She knew that he would have to come all the way into Chicago, to come to her, something he had rarely done during their affair.

PHIL IS EARLY and self-conscious. Behind the maître d's stand he can see his reflection in the mirror, and he moves so that he isn't directly in front of it. A large man in a black open-collared shirt asks him if he can help. "I'm waiting for someone," Phil answers.

"Do you want to wait at a table?"

"Yes."

Phil follows him to a semi-secluded four top in the corner, not far from the kitchen. The maître d' hands him the wine list and puts two menus down, and before leaving the table he takes Phil's order for a pinot noir. The kitchen door pops open and Phil hears metal clank and the pop and rush of frying oil. He watches through the window at the front of the room, desperate for a drink. Then, finally, he sees her. She stops to smooth her skirt before pulling the glass door open.

A moment of glare from outside blocks her face from his view, and he can only see the top of her head, her dark hair in a halo of light. Then she moves and he can see the skin of her lips stretch in a smile. She has her hand out to him, as if to shake his, but he reaches for her cheek, awkwardly, brushing it with his lips. It seems to take her by surprise.

"I'm not late, am I?" she asks.

"No, no!" He smiles. He can't help his enthusiasm; he is so happy to see her grinning at him. He doesn't want to chase her away. "I think I am early."

"I'm sorry you had to travel so far, but I like this restaurant," she says.

He nods. After all the evenings they spent together, eating in hotel rooms, or even an occasional picnic along the river, far from his house, he has never known what her favorite foods are.

"I see you've already ordered something to drink. I know what you like. Do you know what I like?"

"I suppose a chardonnay. Tell me about your new job."

She smiles and looks down at the tablecloth. Phil watches her large oval eyelids and thinks that they are smooth and beautiful.

"The hours aren't always great. But I have stretches of free time to see people and I have a social life now. I didn't have much of one before. I grew tired of the complications of traveling so much for work." She smiles as she makes eye contact with him.

He feels she is in control of the conversation, that she knows what she is doing as they wait for the next thing to say. Sarayu appears more confident than he feels, though he could be wrong. Is she nervous at all, or sorry that they are here? He takes a moment to recover from these thoughts, and to concentrate on what he should say to her that would endear him to her, something small and even meaningless, not the real drama in his life, not his parting from his wife. He is brought back to the immediate. "Other than that, I hang out with friends. Nothing too exciting," Sarayu says. "What about you? You are getting a divorce?"

Phil shrugs. "I don't see much of my family right now. Jilly is still at school, and Isabel spends her time with her mom."

"Linda?"

"The almost-ex? She stays out of the house when I am there in the daytime. She is getting her own place. The girls will spend the summer living in both houses. I may see them more."

"Of course, it won't be like it used to be. Your daughters are grown up. They don't want to stay at home and hang out with their dad."

Phil laughs and shakes his head.

"You know what I mean. Tell me you wanted to stay home all the time with your parents when you were a teen."

"You're right. I didn't."

She touches his arm lightly, then pulls her hand away. "Where is Linda looking for a house?"

"Same town. Same neighborhood. It's a small town and she seems to have taken all of our friends." He laughs to make it seem like a joke, when it really isn't one. "It's all fine. I'm busy with work and the vegetable garden. And keeping up the old workout schedule."

"I can see you're still doing that."

"Keeps my mind clear."

The waiter brings Sarayu's wine, a basket of bread, and takes their orders. Normally this would be a time where Phil would make a toast, but to what? Here's to admitting faults and moving on? So, he tells her about work and how difficult it is in the recovering economy to get businesses to sign maintenance contracts, to bring in new clients, that earlier in the year they had had to lay off two of the women in the office. By the time their food comes, they are on their second glasses of wine and Sarayu begins to pick at the food on her plate, something he has never seen her do. He is struck by this sign of vulnerability, the sort of thing he sees his wife do. He realizes that he has been talking too much, and that he has not told her that he is sorry for the way he treated her in the past. He looks up from his plate. She smiles in a way he remembers.

"I don't mean to take up all the airspace," he says.

She shakes her head as if to say that it isn't a problem.

"Do you come to this restaurant a lot?" he asks.

"Yes. It's only a few blocks from my apartment. My girlfriend used to date the chef." Sarayu takes a small mouthful of food. She chews. There is another space in the conversation, and Phil watches her and waits for her to say something else. She looks at him, then down at her plate. "She is still friends with him, even though they don't go out anymore. So, it's not awkward when she comes here to eat."

"That must be challenging," Phil says.

"You know, I have regretted what happened," he says.

She looks surprised. Her eyebrows crease. "Which part?"

She is angry, he thinks. "No, no! I don't mean the relationship. I can tell by your face that you think I'm talking about the affair. I don't regret that, except that it upset my wife. I regret breaking up."

She drinks her wine.

"And I'm sorry," he says. "I didn't want to hurt you, and I handled it badly. But I didn't know how to handle it."

Sarayu puts her fork down. She sits back. "It's not like you haven't broken up with your mistress before."

He is surprised at her retort. He didn't see the punch coming and he didn't expect her to have this attitude now that they were meeting to have dinner.

"And you didn't do it on your own," Sarayu says. "I was there as well."

He begins to smile with embarrassment. "Yes, you were," he says quietly. "But I didn't mean to hurt you. I'm so sorry I did."

Sarayu looks at the small pile of food she has made on her plate. "I have never understood why people meet at restaurants over meals to discuss significant and unpleasant things. It ruins the meal. It ruins your appetite."

"I didn't want to ruin the meal."

"Then what is all of this?" She spreads out her hands to show the length of the table. "This idea to meet? Was it your idea or mine? I don't remember. I chose the day and time and place. And it isn't like we used to eat out at many restaurants. You hid me away in hotel rooms."

He shakes his head. "I am so sorry."

"Am I supposed to sit here and listen to your divorce story and feel sorry for you? Am I supposed to take some responsibility for your wife wanting to leave you? Because whatever was wrong between the two of you was wrong before I came along."

Phil has nothing to say now.

"I can't do this." Sarayu is looking him in the eye with an unwavering expression. "I thought I wanted to see you. But I can't finish a meal with you."

Then she begins to lose her composure, at first in a small, quiet movement as her locked gaze breaks and she looks at her hands in her lap. He expects her to rise up and leave the table, and he breathes deeply to prepare himself for this public rejection and embarrassment. Then she puts her face into her hands and begins to tremble. Her trembling accelerates. He looks at the leftover food on her plate, and when she begins to sob, he says to her, "Let me take you home. Just walk you to your apartment and see that you get inside."

"I hate crying," he hears her say into her hands. She is embarrassed.

He gets up from the table and walks to the maître d' to pay. "I'm sorry," he says as he signs the credit card receipt. Sarayu looks up and begins to wipe her wet face with her napkin. He takes her gently by the elbow and leads her out of the restaurant.

She doesn't speak as they progress down the block. They approach her building. A cooling wind moves amidst the leaves on the large full trees. Sarayu walks upright. Her shoulders and bare arms are even. She leans into him, then pulls away. "It's ok," he tells her quietly. "I'm just walking you home." He knows she probably feels humiliated, and it hurts him at the center of his chest. He is the reason for her discomfort.

THE DRIVE HOME feels long, but as he pulls into his driveway, he is thinking about Sarayu, walking side by side to her apartment, taking her hand as he said goodbye, he said that he missed her. Then, her whisper, a crackling voice, the kind that betrayed a terrible discomfort, she said that she still loved him. And they parted. At home, his daughter and wife are asleep. He goes to his bed, undresses, and climbs beneath the bedclothes. For the next four hours he falls into a deep and dreamless sleep, the kind he has not had for a long time.

19

KAYE OPENS THE door to a skinny young man with a soul patch and full lips. "Yes?"

"I'm looking for Clara?" he says, tentatively. "Does she live here?"

"I'm her mother."

He stands on the concrete landing below where Kaye has opened the porch door. They are eye level. He seems old for Clara, maybe twenty-five? And it's two thirty in the afternoon. Clara is still at school.

"Is she home?" the young man asks.

"Who are you?"

"I'm Jared. I arranged to meet her here."

"She's seventeen, Jared."

Jared's pale face turns scarlet. He palms his shaggy blond hair and looks at his shoes. "Sorry?"

"She's still at school right now. She's not due to come home for another hour." Kaye reminds herself that the legal age in Illinois is seventeen. "Did she tell you that she is a high school student?"

"Oh no." His hands are now in his front pockets. "I'm not her boyfriend. I'm here about the room. The room for rent.

Are you the one renting it out? It was listed on Craigslist? A room in northwest Evanston? Not far from the football stadium? Near a bus stop? With kitchen privileges?

"What room? I'm not renting a room." Kaye briefly considers actually renting the room. She will be rid of Clara in a year when she goes to college. Maybe it would be better to have a lodger than a daughter who hates her?

"She put her room on Craigslist?"

"I suppose it isn't for rent, then."

Kaye had always thought teenagers were idiots with undeveloped brains, trying to operate as if they knew what they were doing. She isn't changing her philosophy, but momentarily she is almost impressed at what her daughter has done to express how much she hates her. What has happened to the girl who cried when Kaye left her at preschool to fend for herself, because Kaye wanted time off from playing with Clara, from watching to make sure she didn't do anything dangerous, from seeing that her small brain was constantly stimulated while Kaye's own couldn't concentrate on a book. It wasn't *her* idea to have a kid, Kaye thinks, it was Eric's.

Kaye is furious. How far did Clara think this joke would go? Should she call Eric at work? "Did you make an appointment with her over the phone?"

He looks blankly at her, as if waiting for an apology. "Email."

"It's strange she would give you this time."

"I'm early. I walked all the way from campus. I didn't know how long it would take."

"I appreciate that," Kaye says. "But there is no room for rent."

Jared begins to turn around. "Thanks anyway," he says as

he walks down the path.

Kaye watches him leave. At least he was polite, she thinks. She runs to Clara's room. It is easy to guess Clara's computer password, for it is the name of her beloved Scottish grandmother who passed away ten years ago of lung cancer. She came to visit every summer and would sit in the screened porch puffing on the Marlboros she picked up in the airport duty-free shop. Janet. The same password Eric uses. Such a clever twosome, Clara and Eric.

Kaye is waiting in the kitchen when Clara arrives home an hour later. She has been waiting there, drinking coffee, and her stomach is feeling sour from the third cup as she hears Clara's key in the door. "Come in here!" she says in her loudest voice.

"Hold on. I have to go to the bathroom." Clara sounds calm to Kaye.

Kaye stands at the sink and washes the coffee pot, listening for Clara's footsteps. She puts the pot and the mug in the drain just as Clara steps into the doorway. "Tell me about Jared. And Craigslist."

"Shit. I forgot about that."

"He was early. You were still at school. What were you planning? I went to your computer and found that you had taken pictures of your bedroom. You posted them on Craigslist and tried to rent it out!"

"You were on *my* computer?"

"It wasn't difficult."

"That's private. God, you are such a bloody bitch! I can't believe you would go on my computer."

"His name was Jared. He came all the way out here from Northwestern to look at the room. You made an appointment with him. Were you drunk when you set this up?"

"No. I'm not like you."

"What are you talking about?" The bottom falls from Kaye's stomach. "I am not a drunk."

"Believe what you want." Clara looks at the ceiling, then at her mother.

"Don't you talk to me that way."

"Why? What do you ever do for me? You hang around the house hiding all the time. It's not like you watch what I am doing. You never pay attention. You are *so* fucking self-absorbed."

"I am not having this conversation with you if you talk to me like that."

Clara turns and begins to walk away. "One more year and I am out of here," she calls back.

Kaye leans back against the counter. She doesn't know what to do or say. It isn't the first time. The next thing she hears is the front door slamming shut.

WALKING UP THE parkway to her front door, Eleanor writes an imaginary email to Phil. "Dear Phil: I'm sure we can be 'just friends,' except that I have this image of you naked and limp in the darkness of my garage. It's not something I want to think a lot about. So how would this work?" She climbs the porch steps, past the place where she sat with Phil, where she kissed him.

The street is quiet and dark with the long shadows of clouds. A tall thin woman holding a cigarette between her fingers in one hand, and a leash in the other, walks her vizsla on the sidewalk. She takes a long drag near Eleanor's front lawn as the dog sniffs for a place to relieve himself. She smiles and waves the cigarette hand at Eleanor.

Inside, Eleanor's house is quiet. It's late in the afternoon, and she assumes Eugene, home from school, is doing his homework. Liam appears on the stairs. "Can I go to Pete's house?"

Immediately she wants to say no. So, she does, not because she has a reason, but because she feels tired and light-headed, and it just comes out of her mouth.

"Why not?"

"I said so."

"Give me a reason."

"I don't have to. Don't you have homework?"

He retreats, stomping up the stairs.

In her bedroom, she takes out her laptop and sits on the bed. "Dear Phil: It isn't that I don't want to be friends. I don't know how. What do I do now? Mostly I find you sexually repulsive. Yet, if I'm honest, I'm also still attracted to you, perhaps the problem is that I can't get the garage incident out of my head and I can't stop being angry. At me. At you. Should I just ignore you?" She knows the answer to this. Delete.

PHIL WAKES UP in a strange bed, and for a split second, even with the late afternoon sun hitting him in the face from the open window next to the bed, he wonders where Sarayu is, and he almost thinks that he can smell her apartment as he did two nights ago, then realizes that he is in the guest room of his own house, the room his wife has taken. He is lying on top of her bed. He remembers that she wasn't home and he had decided to look through her things, not for anything in particular. He discovered that she didn't fold her underpants and bras, but just put them in the drawer. Her socks lay in an unmatched mass. She hung her T-shirts on hangers rather than place them in the dresser. And her jewelry she had tangled in multiple cotton-lined boxes piled on a shelf in her closet, instead of in the wooden jewelry box he had once given her as an anniversary present. Some of the more expensive pieces he could not find. Not that he cared. His search had been tiring and he had picked up a book, lain back on the bed, and fallen asleep.

As he surfaces into full consciousness, he senses the familiar sourness, a combination of sweat and scented hair products, the pillow she uses, and the blanket.

For a moment he stays there and feels the wind from the ceiling fan across his face. He hears the voices of his neighbors in their yards outside, but there is no one else in his house, only the overhang of disappointments. He stretches as he stands up, then straightens the blanket on the bed so that it doesn't look like he has been there.

In the adjoining bathroom, amidst the body washes and rose-scented soap, he sees the reflection of lines that reach from the outside corners of his eyes toward the sides of his face, and grey circles beneath his white lower lashes. No matter how hard he works out, or how careful he is with what he eats, the years draw the skin on his face downward.

On the table by the bedside are two Bibles, one a new annotated version with the sticker label of her church at the bottom of the front cover, the other her confirmation King

James version. There is a pencil for her to write in the margins of the Bible, and her iPad. He turns the iPad on and, using an old password that Linda had developed, the middle names of their daughters, he logs into her account and looks at her email. How odd it hadn't occurred to her to change her password.

Phil had always felt that it would never really be important to see what Linda had in her email account or on her Facebook page. After all, he was the one committing adultery. It was always Linda accusing Phil. Phil left her alone to raise her daughters. Phil forced her to move just as she was beginning to make friends in one place, and then move again. Phil had affairs, and not just one. She had always been victimized by his actions and his life.

There are emails about clothes and dating from Linda's divorced friends, sort of "Let me set you up" emails; notices about Bible study; love letters from Albert, the man-boy from church. "I can't wait to see you," he writes. "I only want to lie next to you." He quotes songs that Phil is not familiar with. Some are in Spanish, as if that is a sexier language than English. Then he sees the "sent" files, the emails to Sarayu and Eleanor where Linda writes, "I'm praying for you."

He walks through the hallways as he reads them. Now a few things make sense. To Sarayu there is a particular recent email. And now he knows why she called him, because she had heard from his wife.

"He is all yours," Linda wrote. "We are finally getting a divorce. I won't hide the fact that you were partly to blame. But it takes two."

Why did Linda contact Sarayu? To get them back together? It reminds him of twelve-step programs that force you to apologize to everyone you have hurt while you were an addict, and she is apologizing for him. But Linda does not feel she has hurt anyone. She only says she will pray for them. Is praying for someone the same as interrupting her life with information she might not want? Did she think Phil would find out and then hate her? Would it make her superior to Phil, by praying for those he has sinned with?

He sends a text to Sarayu. He sits and waits for an answer. She doesn't answer and he calls, only to find that her telephone is turned off. He wants to reassure her that he is sincere in wanting to be with her.

Phil feels he has to get to Sarayu. He grabs his wallet and keys and gets in his car. He has not thought to let out the dog or fill her water bowl. She doesn't exist right now. At a stop sign before entering the ramp to the expressway, he sends Sarayu another text. Still she doesn't answer. He calls and leaves another message. Her phone is still off.

KAYE DOESN'T THINK it is unusual that Clara has walked out. Clara walks out all the time. Eric believes that Clara should have the freedom to leave the house to be with her friends after school, to calm down after the frequent arguments she has with her mother. Clara communicates with him. Often Kaye doesn't know where Clara is eating, or where she is getting her homework done. Eric, who grew up in a different place, says, "She comes home at night, what more do you want?" as if he knows something that he and Clara don't want to reveal to Kaye.

"How the hell do you raise kids in Scotland?" she asked her husband.

"We don't chain them to their bedrooms, if that is what you are wondering."

Eric does not make things easier.

Kaye does what she always does in the late afternoon of a weekday, before Eric comes home. She empties the dishwasher, marinates the chicken, washes the lettuce for a dinner salad, and indulges in a finger of fifteen-year-old whisky. An advantage to being married to a Scot is that there is always fifteen-year-old whisky in the pantry.

Then the clouds come over the sky, shadowing the ground, and from the kitchen window she can see the tree swing moving maniacally and the huge branches from the cottonwood sway. The siren goes off. Kaye sends a text message to Clara. Then she calls her. Clara rarely answers when her mother calls. The rain begins to pelt the windows, sharply at first, then in waves in an uneven rhythm that coincides with gusts of wind. What little she feels she has of maternal instinct she rallies. She takes her rain jacket and keys and runs toward the car parked in front of the house.

By the time she has crossed the parkway and reaches her car, she is drenched. Would Clara seek cover? Was she at someone's house? Would she find the house of a friend? Clara has been known to walk for hours when she is angry. Kaye sends another text before starting the engine. "Clara, where are you?" She receives no answer.

With the neighborhood siren sounding from the nearby schoolyard, Kaye goes after her daughter. The wind rocks the car and the rain pushes against the windshield. She drives slowly along the street, clutching the steering wheel, trying to see ahead through the watery windshield glass. Up a street, down another, no one is outside. A squirrel runs in front of the car, but she doesn't brake and she doesn't hit it.

She finds Clara soaked and hovering on the grass, not far from the house. She pulls the car up to the curb and reaches to open the passenger side door. "Get in!"

But Clara shakes her head. "Why?" she says.

"It's dangerous! The sirens are going off!" Kaye screams to her daughter. Realizing that she will have to get out of the car and force Clara to get in, she pushes her door open, and, through the shower, she walks over the grass and takes Clara by the shoulders. The girl resists. "Just leave me alone, you fucking cunt!"

Kaye remains standing in the rain and wind. She recalls the time she couldn't get Clara to latch on as a baby and she was trying to nurse. Through the pain of being rejected and her tears, she argued with the lactation nurse to allow her to use formula rather than breastfeed. But the lactation nurse was adamant, and she pinched and pumped milk until the stubborn baby Clara drank from her breast and Kaye contracted a painful infection. Even before that, there had been the pain of contractions, of childbirth, things she had forgotten. Kaye hadn't known what pain was then.

With all the things that Clara has called her she has never used the word "cunt" before, a hard-sounding word, shot out in the hope of injuring her. But words don't matter right now. "Just get in the car and I'll worry about what you think of me later."

"No! I am staying here."

"You'll get hurt. Come!"

Clara tries to wriggle out of her mother's clutches, but without enough energy to be successful. Soaked and tired, Kaye leads her into the car. She pushes the door shut and goes to the driver's side. She cannot hear the sound of the engine, only the pounding of the rain on the car and the blood in her head.

Clara runs through the unlocked front door ahead of her mother when they arrive home. Kaye stands in the doorway listening to Clara slam her bedroom door shut. Then she can no longer hold her tears. They come out harshly, along with seventeen years of failed motherhood.

20

THE STORM COMES on suddenly, as Midwestern spring storms do, and the sky darkens to make it seem as though it is dusk. Frank has just walked into the house from the commuter train. "Eleanor!" he calls out to her. "The trees are bending!"

Frank's "I'm saving the family" act comes about every so often, when there may be a world crisis, when the sewers need rodding, or the bushes in the garden need to be trimmed, or the cars need to be moved to the other side of the street for street cleaning. But this tone is more serious. She can see the sky and the bending branches outside the window, as he goes to the backyard to cover the grill and take down the patio umbrella. He tries to grasp the pole; his hair is wet and flat against his head and his shirttail blows behind him. He cannot hold the umbrella pole, and it shoots off into the air. He runs back inside. "Where is Annie?"

The boys make it slowly into the basement. Eleanor cannot find the dog. Feeling panic, she looks inside closets and behind furniture. She calls out her name as the sky opens and rain pours down. Outside she pushes toward the fence and finds the gate bent. "Did you have her outside with you?"

she calls out to Frank, who is crawling along the side bushes, looking for a place she might hide.

"I don't remember, I think so."

"Well, she's out."

"You go inside and I'll find her," Frank says. "Go into the basement with the boys, I'll find her."

"It's dangerous—"

But he is gone. Eleanor shouts Annie's name and the sound pushes back to her with the wind. The rain slashes sideways through the air and prevents her voice from projecting. Her head is soaked and she can only see vaguely through the drops across her eyeglasses. She looks for the black-and-white dog under trees and on porches as she moves across the sidewalk. She tries to push ahead. Yet the wind forces her back. She can hear the crack and whoosh of a tree branch crashing down somewhere along the parkway into the street. "Frank!" she calls out. "Annie!"

Please be safe, she thinks, longing to hold Annie's wet spindly body and to bury her nose in Annie's neck fur; she cannot bear it if something were to happen to Frank, nor could she stand it if they did not find the dog. She weaves in and out of bushes in the wind and pouring rain, looking in the undergrowth of front yards, expecting to find a wet dog curled in a ball shivering, her eyes red and wide, panting. She sees nothing. Then, turning toward her own home, she finds Frank with his hair plastered to his face and his clothes clinging to his skin, holding the petite, frightened border collie to his chest. Eleanor runs against the rain and falls into them, clutching them both with her arms. Annie smells like new wet wool and tilled soil. "Let's go home," Frank says. Eleanor is overwhelmed with relief.

In the basement, the four of them lie on the painted cement floor under the Ping-Pong table, surrounded by the dirty towels that had lain in a laundry basket. They listen to a transistor radio, reports of traffic accidents and train delays. Frank clings to the dog, whose head is beneath his chest and whose body moves with each quick breath, her tail beating against the floor. The boys are on their backs with their phones, dry, heads propped up on a rolled carpet. They send messages out to the world about their captivity, and report to their friends in other basements. All of them hear branches knock the sides of the house and rain pelt the above-ground basement windows, rhythmic, sweeping rushes of sound. Then there is a loud crash outside, which vibrates the walls of the house as though a train had passed, or a small earthquake had occurred, only louder. "Shit!" one of the boys says. Eleanor can't tell which one.

"Do you think a tree fell?" Frank asks.

Eleanor's phone buzzes in her pocket. She is surprised it is still working after she had been out in the rain. She answers it even though she doesn't recognize the number. It's Linda. "Where is my husband? Is he with you?" Startled, Eleanor hangs up.

"What was that?" Frank asks.

Eleanor deletes the call. "I didn't recognize the number."

"Why did you answer?"

"I don't know. I always do."

"I'm going to check outside. Take Annie."

"Don't be stupid."

"Things have died down. Listen."

Eleanor still hears rain on the window panes. "Don't go!"

He takes her hand. "I'll just be a minute." He gets up and

climbs out from under the table. Eleanor pulls the wet dog to her and folds her body around it, still looking up toward the stairs. Then she hears a door slam.

"It was the ash tree!" Frank says as he moves down the stairs toward his family. "It crashed into the middle of the street, taking two cars down with it."

"Anyone hurt?"

"No."

"Whose cars, ours?"

"Mine." He has his hands by his side. "The tree came out of the ground, roots and all. There is a huge hole at the side of our house."

WHEN THE STORM subsides, Eleanor follows Frank, climbing the basement stairs carrying the dog. As they cross the kitchen threshold, Annie jumps to the floor and runs to her crate. Through the windows they see that the umbrella once over their patio table has lodged itself in the chain-link fence that stands between their yard and the neighbor's. There are thin, full-leaved branches strewn across the grass. They walk out the door and around to the front of the house to see what Frank had discovered earlier: the uprooted ash tree that now lies across the parkway, its branches crushing Frank's Subaru. The roots of the tree are exposed, there is now a crater where the tree had stood.

From a distance, the sirens sound. They can hear the slam of the screen door across the street as their neighbor calls to them, "Frank! Eleanor!"

At the same time, Eleanor's phone vibrates. It is Phil's

home number. Phil has never used it to call her before, and she feels a sudden panic that it might be Linda calling again, yet she answers. "This is Linda Anderson, Phil's wife. Is my husband with you? He isn't here and there are storms and a tornado warning."

Eleanor doesn't know what to say. Frank bends over the dead tree. The trunk is as high as his thigh. "Have a look at this," he says to her.

"I'm sorry, who?" Eleanor says to the phone.

"Linda. Phil's wife. Is he with you? I'm worried about the storms."

"You don't live near here."

"He's gone. I'm sure he's in Chicago."

This is an interruption in her life that she resents. "He isn't here. I'm sorry." She hangs up.

To Eleanor, any drama about Phil suddenly feels far away as she looks at the tree on its side, the roots blackened by the dark earth and twisted in the air. A large branch, split along a fibrous, yellow line that breaks the cracked grey bark, lies near the hulk of trunk across the grass. The place where it has split from the trunk of the tree is jagged. Frank circles widely around his car. He can't get close to it because the tree limb blocks the circumference and most of the street. He stands with his hands on his hips, evaluating the damage. "It's a good thing the tree went this direction instead of toward the house."

"It's like Annie knew," Liam says.

Eleanor turns toward where her son is now standing. "What do you mean?"

"She knew to run away from the tree, the danger. Then Dad went to get her back."

Eleanor puts her arm around Liam's back. He is her height now and leans into her, which he hasn't done in a long time. She nods, frightened by the possibility that Annie might have been hurt by the falling branches outside, or taken up in the wind, because she is only thirty-six pounds.

Frank has his hand to his forehead, as if he is thinking of what to do, but there really isn't anything he can do but wait for the city to clear away the tree and then call the insurance company. The car is old. It is the car Eugene is learning to drive. It's the one in which they brought Liam home from the hospital and took Eugene to soccer games. Eleanor suddenly feels sentimental. She is moved by her husband's stance and walks to him. He looks at her, shaking his head as she puts her arms around him. "I'm sorry," she says. She swallows. "I'm sorry."

He shrugs and they stare at the carnage in silence.

WHEN THE STORM comes on, Phil is in the city, not far from Sarayu's apartment. He drives along the four-lane street that takes him east from the expressway exit to where she lives. He can feel he is pushing against the wind in his small sports car. Branches of large trees are bending on the side of the street. Along the sidewalk an umbrella blows, swept up into the air as the man who had been holding it cowers in his coat. Rain slashes against Phil's windshield and he leans his body forward against the steering wheel, trying to see clearly out the window between swipes of the windshield wipers. But all he sees are blurred colors of the cars in front of him through the wall of rain. They all inch forward, trying to force

their way through the thickness of the storm, and thunder
rolls with startling cracks of lightning. Behind him, Phil hears
the crack of a breaking tree limb and begins to worry that
something will hit the thin roof of his convertible.

He has trouble parking in Sarayu's neighborhood, and
with the rain beating down on his roof and windows, it is
difficult to wedge his car between two others. He runs up
the block to her entryway, through the wind and rain. He is
breathing heavily as he pulls the door open and thrusts first
his head then upper body into the foyer. He leans against
the wall momentarily. Outside it is as if water is falling from
the sky in bursts against the rectangles of glass on the door.
Lightning flashes from outside into the dark entrance. He will
explain everything to Sarayu now, about his almost-ex and her
emails, and what is happening in his life. He doesn't want to
hide anything, to keep her in the dark.

Early in the marriage, one of the things that Linda liked
to do when he was gone was rearrange the furniture. At night,
when he was home, on the way to the refrigerator for a glass
of milk, he would often trip or stub his toes. He could never
remember where things had been before he left.

Sarayu does not answer her intercom on his first try. He
looks at the mailbox numbers to make sure he has the right
apartment, and presses the button twice more before she
buzzes him in. Looking up to the second floor, he announces
himself. She is waiting in her doorway with a puzzled look.
"What are you doing out in this weather? You're lucky I was
in."

"I—" Phil does not know what to say. "We have to talk."

Her black hair is brushed away from her face and behind
her ears. He notices her eye makeup, something she would do

when she was going out, but not when she was at home or working. He reaches her and takes her shoulders in his hands, but that is all he dares to do. He is unable to explain himself and he is soaking wet.

"I have someone here." She sounds worried. "Come in and dry yourself.

She brings him a large bath towel from a white hallway cabinet built into the wall. "Here, you can go to my bedroom and take off your wet clothes. Wrap yourself in this."

As he might have done as a child listening to an adult who knew better, he goes to her bedroom and closes the door behind him. He sets the towel on the bed as he takes off all of his wet clothes, then he begins to dry himself with it. *What am I doing?*" he asks himself, hearing the soft voices of Sarayu and another person echo from the living room. He wonders about Eleanor, what did she do during the storm? Did she shelter with her family in her basement while he was driving like a crazy man through the city? Was she cooking dinner and watching the storm through the window? He is overwhelmed with a rush of tiredness.

Phil wraps the towel around his waist and his long pink legs stretch out beneath it. The towel reaches to just above his knee. Carrying his clothes, he leaves the bedroom, padding along the cool wooden floors of the hallway to the main room, where he finds Sarayu seated in a chair by the window, sitting with a man he has never met in the other, matching chair.

Phil doesn't know any of Sarayu's friends. He hopes the man is just a friend. It has never occurred to him that she might have been seeing someone else. Holding the towel with one hand, he presents the other to shake. "Hi. I'm Phil."

"Josh."

They shake and smile. Josh is lanky and makes Phil feel old. Phil touches the crown of his head, at the bald spot, and tightens the towel as he sits on the couch with his knees together. Sarayu laughs. "You look ridiculous," she says to him. "I'm just going to put these wet clothes into the dryer downstairs. I wish I had a bathrobe or something large enough for you to wear." She is still laughing as she leaves.

"So how do you two know each other?" Josh asks.

Phil wonders what he should say. Friends? Dating? How much does Josh know? "We used to go out together," he says. "Some time ago."

"I've known Sarayu forever, and she has never mentioned you. Unless . . . You could be the mystery man from a year ago."

"Mystery man?"

"Someone she was seeing while she was a traveling nurse, toward the end. She wouldn't say much about him. I figured he was married."

"That was me, then."

"Married or a mystery? Or both?"

"A mystery. I'm separated."

Josh smiles and sips from a glass of beer. Phil keeps his knees together and begins to feel cold. "Too bad you got caught in the storm. We heard a tree crash against something, and we probably should have turned on the radio or TV. We were going to go out to a bar. Good thing we hadn't left yet. Were you driving yourself?"

"Yes." Phil looks at his towel. "Then running from the car. It isn't an easy neighborhood to park in, storm or no storm."

"It isn't."

In the uncomfortable silence, Phil hears Sarayu open the door. She is holding a beach towel.

"This is bigger," she smiles. "Should have more coverage than that miniskirt." They all laugh uncomfortably.

When Phil returns in his new towel, there is a beer on the coffee table near where he had been sitting. Sarayu's smile stretches the dark skin of her cheeks.

"That looks more presentable, though I don't think we're taking you to a bar with us," Josh says. "Sarayu, Phil was telling me how you two used to go out."

"You are being mischievous, Josh," Sarayu says. "I bet Phil isn't asking you how we have known each other. We were practically children together in Toronto." She is comfortable and friendly in the way she exchanges looks with Josh and touches his arm. Phil watches them carefully.

Then Phil smiles, feeling he has dodged the proverbial bullet and mostly kept their relationship private. He opens his mouth to say that the whole thing wasn't a big deal, and who can remember specific details, but then he sees the way Sarayu glances at him, warmly, affectionately, and he can't bring himself to say anything that might hurt her. He begins to cross his legs, and feels the air come into the towel and hit the tops of his thighs as he does, and he stops. He is sitting like a school-girl, his knees together, his toes pointed forward. Sarayu brings him another bottle of beer, and he holds it in one hand and places the other on his lap to keep the towel closed.

Josh is looking out the window. The storm has let up, it isn't as dark, but it is still raining. "It seems to have stopped, but I wouldn't go out there just now. I wonder if some of the neighborhood restaurants even have power."

Phil thinks of when he was in the restaurant with Sarayu,

then tries to put it out of his head.

"Thank goodness we have power," Sarayu says.

Josh drinks his beer and grins. "Plus, Phil is practically naked."

Phil laughs in a high-pitched, unexpectedly feminine way. He is relaxing.

Josh and Sarayu hover over a small countertop, preparing vegetables for an intricate salad they seem to have created together in the past. They boil pasta.

Phil watches Sarayu's thin brown fingers, her trimmed pink nails holding the broccoli delicately under the stream of water in the sink, slicing the tomatoes slowly and smoothly into small wedges, and with the flat of her hand brushing the juice and seeds from the cutting board into the garbage beneath the sink. Josh works around her, skimming her back with his hand as he maneuvers from the stove to the refrigerator. Phil looks to see how they touch each other. He is having a live version of one of those dreams where you forget your clothes when you go to school, only it is at Sarayu's apartment and she has another man as her guest, when he had hoped that she would be alone and he could explain Linda's behavior to her. He has to wait for an interminable forty minutes for his clothes to dry and then decide what to do afterward. Maybe go home.

Sarayu retrieves Phil's clothes from the basement and Phil dresses in her bedroom, wondering what Josh and Sarayu are saying with him not there. His jeans are damp, but not soaking wet.

"I rather liked him in the towel," Josh says as Phil emerges from the bedroom and returns to the kitchen.

"How do you feel now?" Sarayu says.

"Better. Thank you."

"We're almost done here," she indicates the salad and bowl of pasta. "Our emergency meal."

Josh hands Phil a pile of plates. They all move toward the dining table in the living room with the food. Dinner is quiet. In this calm, domestic setting, with Sarayu and Josh, Phil is now part of the life Sarayu has without him. He can sense Josh watching him. Mother bird watching the nest. He has interrupted Josh and Sarayu's evening together. He had never before cared about other people in her life, as long as she was there for him when they met. Here, he is sinking into it, stuck, unable to climb out. They chat about nonsensical things and clean up the dishes together amicably. Josh puts the food away and knows where everything goes. Sarayu opens another bottle of beer and puts it next to Phil. "After drinking this, you will have to stay tonight," she says. It puts Phil at ease that she does not have a romantic connection to Josh.

Then, finally, Josh says that he has to go. "I have to make sure a tree hasn't bashed my sun porch," he says.

Sarayu begins to go toward the hallway and the front door. "No," Josh says, "You finish up here. Let Phil show me out."

Phil wipes his hands on his pants and follows Josh through the hall, past the closet and the bathroom and the bedroom, and Josh stops before turning the bolt on the front door. "I hardly know you, Phil. But I do know the role you played in Sarayu's life, and I don't want you to hurt her again."

Phil is silent. He has nothing to say but looks Josh straight in the eye. "I won't hurt her again."

"Don't." Then Josh smiles forcefully and leaves. Phil stands at the door and closes it, clutching the knob, annoyed. He is overcome with tiredness. It washes over him like a wave. He turns to the kitchen, floating along the wood floor in his bare feet. He finds Sarayu wiping the countertop with a washcloth. Where he once would have carried her off to the bedroom, he waits. He does not know what to do now.

SARAYU OPENS HER eyes. It's barely morning, and the darkness is violet around the room, with a thin line of light emerging through the side of the bedroom curtains. She moves her arm and elbows Phil, accidentally, and as she feels his skin, warm and damp next to her, she begins to remember that he stayed the night. He snores softly beside her. She traces imaginary lines on his back with her index finger and notices that, even though she woke in the middle of the night, unable to sleep next to him, she feels tender toward him where she once could only feel hurt. She moves her face toward his skin, which almost seems to glow in the pale morning, and breathes in his scent, a deep sourness that she had come to enjoy a long time ago and has missed.

She throws her legs over the side of the bed, stands, and stretches her arms to the ceiling, watching Phil's body move with each breath. She finds herself smiling absentmindedly. In the bathroom, she sees the condom floating in the toilet water, and flushes it away before sitting on the seat. When she is finished, she washes her face and brushes her teeth. She drinks two full glasses of water to wash out the alcohol from last night so that she can go to work later with a clear head. She goes back to the bedroom.

Phil's ice blue eyes are wide open. She can see this when she adjusts to the darkness. He is on his back and his arm is stretched to her side of the bed. "Come back," he says, and she crawls in beside him, her head on his warm bicep. "Isn't this what you wanted?" he asks her quietly. Then she feels his body relax as he slips back to sleep. She closes her eyes and begins to fade into a half-sleeping state, where she imagines that Josh has had words with Phil. It is the sort of thing Josh would do, warn away her boyfriends, after flirting with them, almost hitting on them, then telling them to be careful of her feelings. But this time, there is something in what Josh says that is correct about Phil. Phil is vulnerable, still married, still living in the same house with his wife. There are things she needs to discuss with Phil before launching into another relationship with him. Phil isn't thinking straight now. He is needy, and here she is, after a long period of trying to get over him, here she is once again.

21

PHIL PACKS THE hardback copy of Julia Child, an old birthday present to Linda that she never used, a button-down shirt, nice shoes, a new pair of jeans, and his favorite Italian cologne into his duffle and pulls the zipper closed. He is going to stay with Sarayu for the weekend. He hopes that he can cook for her, or that they will cook together. He has picked green beans, lettuce, and asparagus from his garden and put them into a single-handled cooler. He has not discussed his cooking plan with her, but in the past, she has been open to his suggestions.

The relationship is moving forward and Phil is pleased about it. They rely on texting when she is busy working, with no time to talk, or when Linda is in the house. He admits that this gives this new part of their relationship the same edge of being forbidden that existed in the past. He has explained to Sarayu that it is Linda's idea to leave the marriage. She knows they are still in the same house. They both acknowledge Linda's part in bringing them back together.

Linda stands guard at the front door as Phil leaves. He stops at the threshold of the entryway. "What?"

Linda glares at him. She wears her arms folded across her chest. "What about the dog? Who is going to take care of it?"

"She's the *family* dog," he says.

"She is *your* dog and I don't want to take care of her."

Phoenix is not in sight. Phil assumes that she has sought out the back of her crate as she always does when he and Linda raise their voices. "Isabel will take care of her. She knows what to do if you"—he hesitates—"don't." Now he is concerned about Phoenix. Isabel is a fairly responsible teenager. She doesn't get into trouble. And Linda has never shown that she doesn't like the dog.

He stands at the doorway with his duffle in one hand and the cooler in the other. "What's the deal, Linda?" he asks. "You want to move out, but you haven't yet. Do you want me to move out? Because I feel I need a life right now. I can't continue in this limbo, tripping over all of your stuff, and having you around every corner hissing at me and giving me dirty looks. I definitely can't have you calling up potential girlfriends and trying to manipulate my life that way."

Linda moves to the side silently. He slams the door as he leaves. In the car he texts Isabel about the dog. She can handle it. Then he backs his Spider down the driveway.

The drive to Sarayu's is slow. He tries to put Linda out of his mind because he doesn't want the distraction, the aggravation. By now, rush hour is on. He calls Sarayu from the car to say that he is running late.

"Phil?"

"I'm sorry. It's taking some extra time."

"Is it your wife?"

"No. No," he says. But he thinks of her standing at the door. He can't stop her. He wonders who she will email now,

Sarayu, even Eleanor. Right now, there is nothing he can do about it. "I don't know. I don't know," he says on the phone to Sarayu.

"She was upset that I was leaving the dog behind."

"Isn't it the family dog? You can't bring a dog here. They're not allowed in the building.

"No, no. The dog is at home. Linda needs to move out, take her pills, get a massage." He wonders, is he telling her too much? But he wants to be honest this time around, not leave out details that could get him into trouble later on.

"It's okay that you are late, Phil. I'm home from work. Just get here when you can."

"You don't have mood swings, do you?" he asks, laughing at his own joke.

But her tone is guarded. "No, of course not."

"I'm just kidding, you know that."

"Is it going to be this way every time you visit, the arguments with your wife? I don't see why she even has to know." She isn't shrill, or loud, or angry. "Just get here when you can. I'll be waiting."

PHIL DRIVES AROUND Sarayu's block three times before another larger car moves out of a parking space, five buildings away from hers. The Spider fits easily. Phil is becoming more adept at the parking game with each visit. He carries his cargo to her vestibule and presses the button next to her mailbox. "I'm here!" he says loud enough for the entire hallway beyond the glass door to hear him. He senses the vibrations of her footsteps on the carpeted stairs, pausing at the landing before coming down to open the door. The suspense is now over.

She has no expression on her face when he first sees it, as if she needs to register his arrival. Then her lips spread into a smile, and she says softly, "Here you are."

He reaches over through the open doorway and takes her mouth with his and kisses her.

"What is all of this?" she says pointing to the cooler.

His face burns with embarrassment. "I thought we could cook."

"But I have things ready for dinner."

"It's all right. We'll do it another time. No worries." He actively tries not to show his disappointment.

Inside the apartment, they unload. Phil hangs his shirts in Sarayu's closet, then turns as he feels her present.

"You brought vegetables for an army. I'll never finish them. You could ask first."

"I didn't think you'd mind." He smiles and takes her shoulders before moving past her to the hall and the kitchen. "Share it with your friends. Share it with Josh." He opens the refrigerator and sees the six-pack of his favorite beer, which he believes she has bought for him. He looks at her and raises his eyebrows, inquisitively. She nods. "Go ahead," she says.

"Thank you."

"Next thing you know you will be logging on to my computer," she says, smiling.

"I'd tell you if I did that."

"Before or after?"

"Pull this off," he says, reaching for her T-shirt and lifting it away from her torso.

She does and he puts the beer down and traces the aureole of her left breast, which is round and wrinkled as she shivers. "Your hand is cold from the beer bottle. Just take what you want, Anderson," she says, smiling.

He laughs.

>>──<←──>←──>>──<←

PHIL FINISHES THE beer he has left, which is now mildly warm. He wants to shower, but Sarayu is in the bathroom and he does not want to get involved in showering with her right now, so he gets up and puts his clothes on and goes to the kitchen.

In the refrigerator, he notices bowls wrapped in clear plastic and through the film of the wrap he can detect something with pasta and a green lettuce salad, items he hadn't noticed before when he took the beer out. He pictures her cooking with Josh as she had on a previous visit, when he was the outsider, the way they moved in synchronization, reading minds, maneuvering around each other's bodies as though they had done it many, many times. It was something he had once seen himself doing with her, the way he used to cook with Linda, a long time ago.

There are two bottles of cold chardonnay resting on their sides, condiments, plain and flavored low-fat yogurts. She must eat like Linda. No meat, though he has seen her eat meat before. They will have to go shopping if he is to stay here. He searches the cabinets until he finds two wine glasses and opens a chardonnay.

Sarayu appears in her robe. "You found the wine."

"I think I found dinner, too, but I didn't take it out yet. You hungry?"

She takes a glass of wine as he proffers it and smiles. "Yes. After the exercise. Starved. Are you taking over my kitchen? Can I at least put my clothes on before we eat?" She is smiling.

Phil shakes his head. "No." He grins. "I mean yes. I'm not taking over your kitchen and you can get dressed."

She leaves, tracing an imaginary line on the wall with her index finger as she walks, a gesture Phil finds erotic. When she returns, dressed, she takes the two bowls covered in plastic from the refrigerator and brings them to the dining table just off the living room area. The table is already set with woven placemats and white ceramic dishes. "I made Chinese sesame noodles with peppers. Is that all right?"

He forces himself to say that it is and watches her uncover the dishes and put out water glasses and silverware. "As long as I don't have to eat with chopsticks."

She smiles. "You have to eat one noodle at a time."

Phil has them make a toast—awkwardly—to being together, sitting with the corner of the table between them. He eats slowly, appreciatively. At least he thinks he does. Sarayu rolls her noodles on to her fork and shovels them into her mouth. She gulps her wine.

"You're hungry," he says.

"I'm happy," she says. "I've been waiting all day. For several things." She grins shyly, a look of mischief, and watches him grin back. It's something he forces because he feels he is taking in the situation. "One of them was food," she says.

"How is Josh?" he asks.

"Why?"

"I don't know. He's your friend."

"He's been my friend for a long time."

"Did he know about me before?"

"A little."

"Hmm." Phil is not sure he wants to know how much she has told Josh. "I don't want him to think that I'm a bad guy."

"Why do you care?"

"I don't know."

"Don't worry about it," she says. "He doesn't know you. How do you feel about washing the dishes and going for a walk?"

They stand next to each other washing, rinsing, and putting away the dishes. Their elbows brush against each other. Sarayu pauses and puts her head against his upper arm, briefly, as if to tell him that she is there. He likes the feel of her cheek on his arm. It's a gesture of affection, the kind he isn't used to right now.

Daylight is long, and, as they walk, Phil takes a while before he moves to hold Sarayu's hand, putting his palm against her back, just between the shoulder blades, as they stroll, then sliding it to the hand closest to him. She grips it at first, and as they move, she begins to loosen her fingers and relax.

A foursome sits at a table outside a restaurant laughing, drinking. Two men pass them, holding hands. Music spills out of a bar where women younger than Sarayu line up in high heels and tall hair. A panhandler reaches out with his paper Starbucks cup and asks for change. "Will you be blessed?" he says to them. Dusk falls and the neon of a restaurant sign stands out in the fading light. As they walk, they are still holding hands.

POSTCOITAL, THEY ARE lying naked on the bed, the blanket and sheets crumpled around them, and the ceiling fan blowing cool air across their bodies.

"Penny?" Sarayu asks.

"What?" Phil answers as if he has barely heard what she said.

"Penny for your thoughts. Didn't your mother ever ask you that?"

"Did yours?" Phil puts his hand behind his head and watches the shadows of the moving fan on the ceiling.

"She did."

"In Indian?"

"What? No, silly. In English. She was born in Toronto. My grandmother is from India. There are hundreds of languages in India."

"I was thinking of how you met Josh."

Sarayu turns on her side. "Again? He is just my friend. That's all. I knew his girlfriend a long time ago, when I was at university. She was my friend. I was young. She was the kind of girl who gets into trouble. I was the one who would try to talk her out of things."

"Like . . ."

"Sneaking into the rec center in the middle of the night to swim after we'd been drinking. We knew someone who worked there and had keys. Decorating a statue of Queen Victoria near the university. Things you do when you are drunk and a student. Except that we weren't always drunk." She turns onto her back. "I don't know where she is now. She and Josh broke up. Then later, I moved here and knew he lived here. I wanted a friend, so I looked him up. That was years ago. And he doesn't have girlfriends anymore."

"Oh?"

"You couldn't tell?"

He faces her. "I guess not."

"Why are you asking me this now? We just made love and you are asking me about another man as though he were someone who I would have a romantic relationship with. Are you suddenly possessive? What if I were to ask you about how many affairs you had during your marriage, before me? And how many you found on the internet?"

"Go ahead." Phil props himself up on his elbow and looks down at her face.

"Well?"

"Do you really want to know?"

"Who did it start with?"

"A woman I worked with. I didn't find her on the internet. We traveled together, worked together. I was unhappy at home. Linda wouldn't have sex with me. I had to do something." He laughs nervously. "You knew about this."

"You told me about her when I met you."

"But now you want to know about other women."

"Why are you laughing?"

"I'm still married."

"And you were when we met."

"Now I'm getting a divorce."

"Come closer. Just lie with me."

"I am close."

"Closer."

He rustles the sheets as he moves the small distance between them and leans in so that their foreheads touch.

"That close enough?"

"Yes." Her eyes are closed. "You can go to sleep now."

"I didn't brush my teeth."

"One night won't kill you. Go to sleep."

"I was about to, but you wanted a penny for my thoughts."

"You really can sleep now. Go on."

"You are distracting me."

"Not for long. I'm falling asleep."

"So am I."

Phil's phone sounds. "That's my daughter's ring." He sits up and reaches for his phone.

"You should answer it," Sarayu says.

"Isabel? Yes? No, I wasn't asleep. What's going on?" He listens. "Wait a minute. Slow down, Isabel. Who? Ok. Ok. I'm coming home. There's nothing you can do now. It's—no, it isn't your fault. Ok. Yes. I'm coming home."

Phil turns to Sarayu. "She let the dog out. She got hit by a car. Phoenix is dead."

"Who let her out, your daughter?"

"No. Linda. Linda let the dog out and forgot about her. She ran into the street to chase cars. The neighbor didn't see her in the dark and she got hit. That was Isabel on the phone. She is with the neighbor."

"I'm so sorry." Sarayu puts a hand on his arm.

Phil gets up and begins to put on his clothes. "I have to take care of this."

"I know how much you loved the dog."

"Not as much as I hate Linda right now."

"You think she did this on purpose?"

"I do."

Sarayu gets out of bed and wraps herself in her bathrobe. "Is she that crazy?"

Phil is buttoning his jeans when he stops to meet her eyes. "I have tried to tell you that it is a volatile situation!" His tone is dead serious and he is angry. Sarayu doesn't like the way he is looking at her, as if, for the moment, he sees Linda in her. It isn't an experience she has had with Phil. She backs away. "I don't want to have to explain this again," he says to her. "You know how it is."

"I am not sure that I do. I'm not sure I understand your baggage." She leaves the bedroom and goes into the bathroom to catch her breath. She turns on the water in the sink and cups her hands to toss water on her face, then buries it in a hand towel. She isn't crying, but she feels as though she has been. When she opens the door, Phil is standing there.

"I'm sorry," he says. He doesn't put his arms around her as she expects him to, but passes her on the way to the toilet, closing the door behind him. When he is done, he packs his overnight bag in the bedroom. "I'm sorry," he says again, and takes out his car keys. He stops to look at her and Sarayu sees that he is all business, a dramatic shift from fifteen minutes ago.

"I'll call you in the morning after I've settled this problem."

She wonders if she should tell him that he has angered her, or say something to comfort him, but she does nothing because she cannot decide. She follows him to the front door.

"This isn't the way we were supposed to end the weekend," he says.

"You are upset about your dog," she finds herself saying.

"Worried about my daughter. Angry at my wife. I don't

know how I am going to talk Isabel down from all of this. Maybe call her from the car." He reaches and kisses her on the cheek. "Again, I'm sorry."

"For talking to me the way you did?"

"What?"

"This isn't about you."

Phil puts his duffle on the floor. "Oh—come on!"

"Don't talk to me like I'm your wife."

"Ok, ok. We can deal with this later, can't we? I have to go. My kid is waiting for me to get home."

She nods. He puts his hand on her shoulder. "Don't make a big deal, not now, please? I have to get through this with Linda."

She nods, but inside she isn't nodding. He leaves. She shuts the door and goes back to bed, but she can't sleep. She lies awake thinking about how things have not changed. Phil is the same. She is the same. No, maybe she is not the same. Finally, she dozes.

At sunrise, which is near five in the morning, she wakes and gets out of bed. She changes the sheets and takes a shower. When she returns to bed, she falls into a deep sleep.

22

ELEANOR ARRIVES THROUGH the gate at the side of the house. She breaks Kaye's concentration as she unloads a Rubbermaid container of margaritas and a bag of blue corn chips from her tote bag onto the patio table. "I'm glad you called," Eleanor says. "No one is at home at my house. I was dying of boredom."

"Me too."

"Any news from Clara today?"

Kaye shakes her head and pours from Eleanor's container into two handblown margarita glasses. "She stays out all day, even getting up early to leave, then comes home at ten when I am asleep. I don't even know how she is doing at school. She talks to her dad. I'm useless."

"Don't say that!"

"Eric thinks we should let her work out her angst on her own. But he wasn't around for the storm. He didn't chase Clara down and find her when the emergency sirens went off. He wasn't frightened like I was. He was downtown working. I was the one who found Clara in the storm. I'm the one she's nasty to. I should leave Eric to raise her and see what happens. It was his idea to have a kid. It was his idea to have me stay at home. It's been rather a failure."

"You're not serious," Eleanor says from inside her margarita glass.

Kaye shoots her a death ray of a look. "She put up her room for rent on Craigslist."

"You haven't told me about this. Did she mean it? How could she do that?"

"We didn't discuss whether she meant it or not. I answered the door in the middle of the day while she was at school and discovered a guy there wanting to rent her room. She is such a stupid teenager that she forgot the guy was coming around. It's such a ridiculously far-fetched idea. I don't know how she could have been serious. But I'm not in her crazed head."

"What guy?" Magda appears at the side of the house. She is carrying a bowl of raw vegetables and she puts them on the table. "This is to counteract the chips." She pours herself a margarita. "Who are you talking about?"

"Clara put her bedroom on Craigslist as a rental," Eleanor says. "A guy came to check it out when Clara was at school. He'd made an appointment with Clara. Kaye answered the door."

Magda laughs until she sees that Kaye doesn't think it's funny. "How typical," she says. She sits at the table. "They are so stupid at that age." Magda's older daughter is now in college. The younger one is Clara's age, but they are not friends.

"I thought he was some guy she'd picked up at a club or coffeehouse who thought she was older. How the hell do I know what she does with her free time. He was in his twenties. I thought she'd lied about her age," Kaye says.

"Then what happened?"

"He left. She came home from school. She left the house. The usual. The storm erupted and I got worried that she was out in it. I chased her down, put her in the car, brought her home. Now she isn't speaking to me. Apparently, she doesn't want me running her life. Or raising her."

"You've already raised her," Magda says.

"Into someone I am not sure I like."

They sit in silence for a moment. Until Magda says, "It won't always be this way. She'll change and get over it. When she needs something. Emotional support. Money. A car."

"She has someone," Kaye says. "She has her dad." She looks at the bottom of her glass rather than at Magda. "Let's talk about something else."

Magda nods. "What's up with the guy from high school?" she asks Eleanor. "The old boyfriend?"

"He wasn't my boyfriend. I just knew him."

"Residual romantic feelings?"

"No."

"He has a daughter at school here, at Northwestern, and one in high school, and he is getting a divorce from his wife. But she still lives with him." Kaye tips back the rest of her margarita. "Not very 'divorce-y' behavior if you ask me, to live in the same house."

"Maybe it's a big house," Magda says.

"I've never been there," Eleanor says.

"Not yet, "Kaye says.

"Not ever," Eleanor says.

"Why? Did the romance flicker out? What happened?" Kaye asks.

"No romance. I got a call from his wife during the storm. She wanted to know if he was here. I told her no," Eleanor says. She blinks and looks away.

"I told you this was going to happen." Kaye sits back and folds her arms against her chest, then leans forward to refill her glass.

"The big storm where you lost your car and tree?" Magda says.

"Yes."

"So where was the guy?" Magda asks.

"How did the wife get your number?" Kaye asks.

Eleanor shrugs her shoulders with a mouthful of tortilla chips. "How should I know. I hardly know this guy or the privacy settings on his phone. The question should be, 'Why is she calling me?' And I don't know the answer to that. It was weird."

"I agree. Although, I could be a police detective and find out." Kaye smiles for the first time since Eleanor has arrived.

"No." Eleanor sounds uncertain.

Kaye swirls the drink in her glass. "Did the city come and chop up the tree that fell in front of your house?"

"So far they have cleared the part of the tree that fell into the street. They measured the trunk and marked the sewer and cable lines. I suppose they will remove the stump. It's huge."

"And Frank's car?" Kaye has successfully changed the subject.

"Towed. Frank wasn't home when the truck came."

"Now you will have a new tree and a new car," Magda says, happily. "Not bad in the end. Someone on my street lost a huge cottonwood that fell into their yard, and their ten-year-old son put up a sign, tours of the dead tree for fifty cents."

"He's lucky no one was hurt or killed when the tree fell,"

Kaye says. They all sit silently for a moment. "Did anyone take the tour?"

"One or two."

"Frank loved that car," Eleanor says. "I feel really bad about the whole thing."

Kaye watches Eleanor and thinks that she means something more than the storm and the tree, but she won't ask her. Eleanor wouldn't answer truthfully, she knows. And now Kaye has her own problems to worry about. She thinks about the little secret suitcase she has had for some time in the back of her closet, packed and ready for the proverbial rainy day. And now, the rain has come and gone, and it feels to her like it is time. She refills everyone's glass distractedly and waits.

SARAYU STANDS IN front of her refrigerator, looking for something else to bring to work with her lunch. There are large green plastic bags of lettuce and green beans from Phil's garden, wilted and rotting. She didn't eat them. She knew she wouldn't eat them when he brought them. She was, however, impressed by Phil's eagerness, the effort he had taken to try to find something besides sex for them to do with each other. He had wanted to cook with her, but she had made dinner before he arrived so that they would not have to waste time cooking. It wasn't her favorite thing to do as a group activity. And in the end, it was good to leave the house and go out walking in the neighborhood, to bring the relationship out in public.

Her home is her sanctuary. It was where she found comfort after he had broken up with her in the past. She is hoping that Phil does not see it as a sanctuary away from his wife.

As he left in the middle of the night to go back home to his daughter, she began to feel that he did. Ever attentive, he had called early in the morning, long after arriving home and sorting his situation. "My daughter is very angry at her mother. She won't speak to her. It's a real mess over here. A real mess. Linda needs to move out."

"I don't know what to say, Phil. I am sorry all of this happened."

It would always be a mess, she thought, if Linda did not go.

A few days later, when she met Josh for coffee, and she mentioned that Phil had visited for the weekend, she saw the muscles in Josh's face tense. She did not want to spend the energy once again explaining everything to Josh and hear him tell her that what she was doing wasn't going to work. She did not tell him that Phil's daughter called, that Phil had left in the middle of the night, and that she felt the whole thing was strange, being in the midst of someone else's divorce. Josh had been right in so many of these circumstances, and she didn't want to hear it again. So, she said nothing more than, "Phil stayed over for the weekend," a brief report that would explain what she had done, and saw that Josh picked up her cue. He did not question her.

She removes Phil's vegetables from the bags and puts them in the garbage, washing the plastic bags and propping them up to dry with chopsticks on the drain board. It was a shame to waste everything.

The time with Phil had not been spectacular before his daughter called about the dog. There were moments of comfort, and the sex was nice. Sarayu didn't bring up the fact that Phil was still not moving forward on the divorce or that his wife had yet to move out, but something like a light switch turned on for her when he left, as if to say out loud that Phil is not divorced yet and may never be divorced. Things have not changed much. The difference is that they are now not hiding in hotels.

All of this feels to Sarayu as though they are fitting themselves into old patterns. Still, she isn't going to bring up her dissatisfaction just yet, not after the drama of losing his dog, she thinks as she wraps her turkey sandwich in plastic and puts it into her lunch pouch.

Phil comes to her with vegetables from his garden that wilt and become inedible. She gathers the trash bin liner, ties the ends, and deposits it in the garbage chute outside her apartment. She is well aware of the symbolism.

Her phone buzzes with a text message from Phil. "Good morning, Gorgeous!" No word about what happened as he left her. Nothing about the dog.

Is this good or bad? Does it mean that it's her job now to call him and ask? Maybe. That is what one does if one is in a relationship. And yet, Sarayu doesn't answer him.

She wonders if she will get an email from Linda. She never answered Linda's last email, and it seems to her that Linda would only contact Sarayu if she had been prompted by a previous response. Yet, Linda will always be in the background of any relationship with Phil. Sarayu doesn't want this. She values her space, her privacy. Maybe this is why she never settled down. Maybe this is why she picked men who wouldn't.

She would answer Phil's text later from the bus. She was in no hurry.

KAYE PULLS OUT the carry-on suitcase from the back of her closet. In it she has kept two pairs of jeans, two blouses, a wool sweater from college, an old winter jacket, socks, shoes, underwear. She fills a quart-sized Ziplock bag with toiletries and goes to the strongbox in her husband's closet to take out cash and her passport. He has five hundred dollars in the box, and she puts these notes, all crisp and new, into her purse.

She has called for a taxi, which arrives twenty minutes early. She locks the front door behind her and asks the driver to take her to the airport. As she explains the best route to take her from her house, she suddenly realizes that it isn't necessary to drive the most efficient way to the airport. She is not on a schedule. She is not coming back.

When the driver approaches the departure drop-off, he asks her which airline he should leave her at. She makes something up. She has no particular destination but selects the terminal from which she can also leave for London, Madrid, and Tokyo, as well as several cities in Canada. Maybe she will purchase a ticket to Toronto.

She lifts her purse and suitcase out of the taxi and hands the driver what she thinks might be twice the cost of the ride, she wasn't paying attention.

She is shedding an old skin.

THE SUN IS out in the morning, and Eleanor takes her coffee to the balcony outside her bedroom. There she sits, checking her morning emails, in the quiet of the space overlooking her backyard and those of the neighbors. There are no sparrow nests now. She had called an exterminator and a man with a ladder came to remove them and repair the pigeon spikes.

When this was all done, she wrote out a check for two hundred fifty dollars.

From her perch, Eleanor writes on her computer.

Hello Linda,

I feel that the time has come for me to tell you not to send me any more email. My friendship with your husband, or ex-husband (whatever you are calling yourselves these days), has come to an end. *Finis.* Over.

I don't know why you spend so much time emailing me with your problems. They are not my problems. Like you, I have a husband and teenage children, and they take up the space in my brain devoted to problems. I have no room for the issues of other people and I am not a therapist. I've only met you once, and at that time you had the wrong idea about my relationship with Phil. You are a physically beautiful woman—far more beautiful than I—but you are a bit twisted, and I don't need that in my life. In fact, I don't need either of you to mess things up for me. What I have is reasonably stable, even if it is a bit dull. So, please, from now on, leave me alone.

She rereads the message. Then presses delete. Then closes the computer.

ACKNOWLEDGMENTS

One can't produce a novel on one's own anymore. I have several people to thank.

First, if it had not been for my husband Brian Ostrow's love and good humor this book would still be in my head.

I would like to also thank Ian Morris, Anne Saywitz, and Joan Slavin for their comments and editing help. Kay Day was my first reader and immensely supportive, always wanting to read more. Pat Skalka, Jeanne Mellet, and Ellen Pinkham helped in ways only the best of writing groups can, critically and emotionally. Mike Ostrow, my web guru, sorted out anything technical, for which I have no skill and am very grateful. Thanks to the editors of *Hamilton Stone Review,* in which an earlier version of some elements of this novel appeared in short story form. And thank you to Deborah Robertson and Gibson House Press for finally creating the published piece.

ABOUT THE AUTHOR

Born in Milwaukee, Wisconsin, and raised in Champaign, Illinois, Esther Yin-ling Spodek is a graduate of the University of Virginia and received her MFA in Creative Writing from Indiana University. Her short stories have appeared in literary magazines and she taught composition at Columbia College in Chicago. She currently lives in Evanston, Illinois, with her husband and border collie.

GIBSON HOUSE PRESS connects
literary fiction with curious and discerning
readers. We publish novels by musicians
and other artists who love music.

GibsonHousePress.com
 GibsonHousePress
 @GibsonPress
 @GHPress

FOR DOWNLOADS OF READING GROUP GUIDES
for Gibson House books, visit
GibsonHousePress.com/Reading-Group-Guides